# Sneak Attack

Clint heard the creaking of the floor out in the hall, and he heard the roof outside his window creaking.

He put his lips near Delilah's ear and said, "When I tell you, roll onto the floor."

"The floor? Why—"

"Just do it!"

Clint reached up to the bedpost and took his gun out of his holster.

The door flew open as someone kicked it, and he shouted to Delilah, "Now!" and pushed her to his left, away from the door.

He turned on the bed and fired at the door, three shots in quick succession.

When he heard the window break, he heard Delilah cry out. He turned and saw the muzzle flash of a gun from the window, as he pulled the trigger of his own gun.

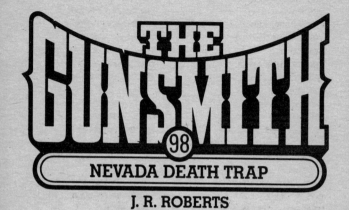

# THE GUNSMITH

## 98

### NEVADA DEATH TRAP

## J. R. ROBERTS

J
JOVE BOOKS, NEW YORK

NEVADA DEATH TRAP

A Jove Book/published by arrangement with
the author

PRINTING HISTORY
Jove edition/February 1990

ISBN: 0-515-10243-1

Jove Books are published by The Berkley Publishing Group,
200 Madison Avenue, New York, New York 10016.
The name "Jove" and the "J" logo
are trademarks belonging to Jove Publications, Inc.

PRINTED IN THE UNITED STATES OF AMERICA
10 9 8 7 6 5 4 3 2 1

# ONE

It had been a good week for Clint Adams.

It seemed as if there had suddenly been a wide-spread plague that had infected many of the guns that existed in Nevada. That may have spelled bad news for the owners of the guns, but for a traveling gunsmith like Clint Adams, it was nothing but good news. He had enough money on him now to be able to take some time off, if he desired to do so. In fact, he had so much money that he was looking for a town with a bank large enough to wire the money to his bank in Labyrinth, Texas.

The last town he'd been in had yielded lots of guns that needed work but had not had a very large bank and they didn't offer that kind of service. They had told him there that the next town, Virginia City, had a very large bank and would be able to do that for him.

He was about five miles outside of Virginia City when he saw the other wagons. One of them was listing to one side, indicating that the right rear wheel was broken. He had never seen such a cluttered wagon in his life. In fact, both of them had so much stuff hanging on the outside that he couldn't even tell what kind of wagons they were. He did know that they were in trouble, though, and he had given up a long time ago the thought that he could ever mind his own business.

There was a group of people around the wagon as he approached, and all were dressed rather... differently. Their clothing was on the gaudy side, some of them had kerchiefs covering their heads, and they were all wearing earrings—even the men.

One word leapt into his mind.

Gypsies.

He had never known any Gypsies before, but he'd heard about them, and if he wasn't looking at some now, he'd eat his hat.

He rode up to them and they stopped what they were doing to stare at him. Two men were underneath the wagon, holding it up, and one of them was very big and looked as if he were taking most of the weight.

Standing alongside were two other men and three women. One of the men was very old, the other very young. As for the women, one was very old, one was very young, and the other one was somewhere in the middle. The old woman had once been very hand-some, the middle one *was* very handsome, and the younger woman—who couldn't have been more than nineteen—was extremely lovely. They all had hair as black as midnight, except the older woman's was streaked with white.

They all stared up at Clint with suspicious eyes, as

if he had ridden up to take something from them.

"Looks like you're having a problem," he said. "Can I help?"

"We can take care of it, thank you," one of the men under the wagon said. He was not the bigger man, but he looked to be the leader. He and the big man lowered the wagon and came out from beneath it.

The spokesman was in his early forties, a dark-haired, handsome man with a strong jaw and a broad chest. He wore a gold earring in one ear. The bigger man was younger, in his late twenties. He was not as handsome, but he had the same strong jaw, leading Clint to believe they were related. The age difference was not enough for them to be father and son, so he figured them for brothers.

It was then he noticed the woman in the middle, who was about thirty and also seemed to have the same jaw. She was probably their sister. He wondered if the older woman and man were the father and mother.

Clint stepped down from his rig and walked over to the wagon. They had hit a large stone and it had cracked the wheel and actually taken a piece out of it.

"Do you expect to be able to patch that wheel?" Clint asked.

"We will fix it," the man said with assurance.

Clint looked at the wheel again. If anyone was going to be able to fix it, it would have to be a professional.

"I don't think so."

"Can you fix it?" the thirty-year-old woman asked.

"No," Clint said, looking at the size of the wheel, "but I think I have a spare that will fit."

"And you would give it to us?" she asked.

"No," he said, "I won't *give* it to you, but I'll loan it to you."

"And what would you want in return for this, eh?" the man said.

Clint shrugged.

"I'd just want you to ride into Virginia City with me, where I would take my wheel back and you could either get yours fixed or buy a new one."

"And nothing more?" the man asked.

"No," Clint said, "nothing."

While the man pondered the offer Clint looked at the women. The young one was boldly looking him over, and he was doing the same to the middle one. He still figured her for about thirty, and her eyes were as black as her hair. Although she seemed to share a family trait with the other men—the jaw— hers was not quite as squared off as theirs were.

Clint looked at the spokesman and saw that he in turn was looking at the older man. He also looked at the older man and saw him nod to the other man. Could it have been the older man who was the leader?

"Very well," the man finally said, "we accept your offer of assistance."

"Good," Clint said. "Could I get some help taking the wheel out of the back of my rig?"

"My brother will help you," the man said, and the bigger man stepped forward and smiled at Clint.

"Let's go," Clint said to the big man.

The big man followed Clint Adams to his rig and waited while Clint stepped into the back and cleared the wheel away.

"I'll get it," the big man said.

Clint stepped down to make room for the big man, who climbed inside.

"You have many guns," the man said, looking around Clint's rig.

"It's what I do," Clint said. "I repair guns and sometimes sell them."

The big man took another moment to look around and then lifted the heavy wheel and stepped down out of the rig with it.

"What's your name?" Clint asked.

"I am Nicholas Roman."

"My name is Clint Adams."

"I am very happy to meet you," Nicholas said.

"Your brother didn't seem so happy for the offer of help."

"My brother is very suspicious of offers of help from people who ask nothing in return."

"Doesn't he think there are people who just want to help other people?"

"No," Nicholas said, "he does not. I must take this wheel to the wagon."

Clint walked behind the man as he *carried*—he didn't just wheel it—over to the damaged wagon. He and his brother set about replacing the wheel, declining Clint's assistance.

"Would you like a cup of coffee?" the older woman asked.

"Yes, thank you."

"Granddaughter," the woman said to the youngest woman, "please see to it."

"Come with me," the young woman said.

"Thank you."

"I will come also," the middle woman said. "It is boring to watch a wheel being changed."

Clint followed the young woman to the other wagon and around to the other side of it, where a fire was going. Clint had not seen the fire before because it had been hidden by the wagon.

There was a pot of coffee on the fire, and a pot of something else that smelled wonderful.

"Would you like something to eat with the coffee?" the young woman asked.

"Yes, I would, thank you," Clint said. "I am kind of hungry."

The woman looked up at the sky, giving Clint a clear look at the lovely line of her neck. She was wearing a dress that covered her from neck to ankles, and he could see that although she was slender, she had proud, thrusting breasts. The other woman, the one who was about ten years older than this one, wore trousers and a shirt that had two buttons open, showing a hint of cleft between her large, rounded breasts.

"It will be dark soon," the young woman said, staring at the sky.

"You will stay and have dinner with us," the other woman said.

"Yes," the young woman said. "You will stay the night."

Clint found himself the object of long looks from both women and wondered if he wasn't biting off more than he could chew, here.

# TWO

Over coffee the two women gave Clint the run-down on who everybody was.

The young woman's name was Julia Miro, and the other woman was Delilah Rome. The young man was William, Julia's brother. He was fourteen.

The big man he had already met, Nicholas Roman.

"Armando is Nicholas's brother," Delilah said, "and they are both my brothers."

"Armando is the one who wasn't so anxious for my help," Clint said.

"You must understand," Delilah said, "there are not many people who offer us help without wanting something in return."

"Something very . . . personal," Julia said.

Looking at the two women, Clint could under-stand that— he didn't condone it, but he understood it.

7

"And what about the, uh, older couple?"

"They are my grandparents," Julia said. "Ivan and Maria Miro."

The names all sounded strange to Clint.

"Strange names?" Delilah asked, as if she could read his mind.

"Ah, yes," Clint admitted.

"I don't blame you," she said. "Next month we might have different names. That is the Gypsy life. A new place, a new name, a new . . . friend."

Her look when she said *friend* was rather suggestive—at least to Clint's eye. Maybe he was just seeing things.

"Anyway," Julia said, "no matter what name they use, my grandparents are the king and queen of the Gypsies."

"King and queen?" he asked. "You have a king and a queen?"

"Oh, yes," Delilah said. "We are on our way to a gathering of our people. They will come from everywhere to sit at the feet of the king of the Gypsies."

"How interesting."

"Would you like to come?" Julia asked.

Delilah looked at Julia sharply, a look that Clint caught even if the younger woman didn't.

"Ah, I'm sure your grandparents would have a lot to say about that, Julia," Clint said, and looking at Delilah, he added, "As well as your brother."

"I am sure they would—"

"Julia," Delilah said, "see to the dinner."

Julia frowned at Delilah but did as she was told.

"She is young," Delilah said. "Her gratitude for your help—"

"I understand," Clint said. "You don't need to explain."

"We really are grateful for your help with the wheel," she assured him.

"It was my pleasure," Clint said. "Could I have some more coffee? It's very good."

"Secret Gypsy recipe," she said. "I am glad you like it."

He was sipping his second cup when Armando Roman came over to the fire.

"Is it fixed?" Delilah asked.

"Yes, it is fixed." Armando leaned over and poured himself a cup of coffee.

"I have invited Clint to eat with us and stay the night."

Armando gave Delilah the kind of look Delilah had given Julia a few minutes before. Delilah noticed it and didn't blink.

"It is the least we can do," she said, "and we do have to go into Virginia City with him tomorrow."

"Ivan—"

"Ivan won't mind," Delilah said. "He will want us to extend our hospitality to Clint for helping us."

Armando stared at Clint this time, who followed Delilah's example and didn't blink.

"There is a stream nearby," Armando said to Delilah. "Nicholas and I will wash for dinner."

"Dinner will be waiting when you return."

Armando dumped the remainder of his coffee into the fire and walked away.

"I don't think he likes me," Clint said.

"He doesn't," she said.

"Why?"

"Because he wants to marry me."

"What's that got to do with me?"

"He knows I have my eye on you."

"He thinks you have your eye—"

She shook her head and said, "He does not *think* I have my eye on you, he *knows* I do."

"You do?" Clint asked.

"Yes," she said, smiling at him, "I do. Does that make you nervous?"

Clint hesitated a moment so she'd think he was thinking the question over and then said, "No, not in the least."

Armando and Nicholas stripped and waded into the stream to get rid of the axle grease they were smeared with.

"We are lucky that Clint came along when he did," Nicholas said.

"I do not trust him," Armando said.

"He did not ask for anything in return," Nicholas said.

"But he will expect something," Armando said. "We will keep a close eye on Mr. Clint Adams."

# THREE

The delicious smell turned out to be coming from something Delilah called a Romany stew.

"Another Gypsy recipe?" he asked.

She smiled and said, "*Secret* Gypsy recipe."

"Ah, I forgot about that," he said. "You Gypsies seem to have a lot of secrets."

"Everyone has a lot of secrets," Delilah said. "I bet you have a lot of secrets, Clint."

"Some," he admitted.

Clint was sitting on one side of the fire with Delilah. On the other side were Nicholas and Armando. Sitting to Delilah's right was Julia, who did seem happy about the arrangements.

Ivan and Maria were taking their meal in their wagon. Clint got the idea that Delilah and Julia slept in the second wagon, while Nicholas and Armando slept underneath one of the wagons.

11

He would guess that Armando preferred to sleep beneath Delilah's wagon.

Clint leaned over and said into Delilah's ear, "I'm getting a lot of unfriendly looks."

"Except from Nicholas," Delilah said. "I think he likes you."

"And Julia?"

"Julia has her eye on you," Delilah said.

"I'm very flattered to have the attentions of two beautiful women."

"No, you are not."

"I'm not?"

She shook her head.

"You are very used to having beautiful women interested in you, close to you—"

"Delilah!" Armando said.

Delilah allowed her eyes to linger a moment on Clint, then she looked at Armando.

"Yes?"

"It is time to go to sleep," Armando said. "Julia?"

"Yes, Armando," Julia said. She tossed Clint a lingering look, then rose and went to her wagon.

"Delilah," Armando said, "we will have to get an early start in the morning."

Delilah looked at Clint and said, "I better go before he makes a scene."

"All right," Clint said. "Good night."

"Where will you be . . . sleeping?"

Clint had thought about that already.

"I think it would be . . . better if I slept away from the wagons. I'll put my bedroll down by the stream."

"You don't sleep in your wagon?"

"Not unless it rains," Clint said. "I prefer sleeping under the stars."

"I don't blame you," she said, standing up. "I like the stars too. Good night."

Delilah went to her wagon and climbed inside.

"We will be leaving very early in the morning," Armando said to Clint, "with or without you."

"I'll be ready," Clint said, standing up.

"If we leave before you wake up, we will leave your wheel in Virginia City, with the smith."

"Don't worry," Clint said, "as much as you'd like to leave without me, I'll be ready. Good night, Nicholas."

"Good night."

Clint went to his rig for his bedroll, and then, as an afterthought, walked Duke down to the stream with him. He wanted to keep the big gelding close by.


Clint stripped to the waist and washed himself in the stream. He had put his shirt back on but had not yet buttoned it when Duke let him know that someone was approaching. His first thought was Armando, sneaking down to stick a knife in his ribs. He lay down on the bedroll with his gun close at hand and closed his eyes.

After a few seconds he heard it, too, somebody's footsteps on the hard ground after they'd stepped off the grass.

He waited until they were bending over him and then brought his gun around and cocked it.

"Oh!" The sharp intake of breath was clearly feminine, followed by the smell of her in his nostrils.

"I'm sorry," Clint said, easing the hammer down and taking the gun away from her nose.

Delilah took a few seconds to catch her breath. Her eyes were wide and the moonlight was reflecting off them. Her breathing was quick, her nostrils flaring.

"Who were you expecting?" she asked.

"I didn't know who it was," Clint said. "I'm just always careful."

"Are you a criminal?"

He smiled and said, "No."

"But you sometimes have people sneak up on you?"

"Sometimes."

She looked down at him then and slid her hand over his chest and belly.

"And not always amorous women, eh?"

"No," he said, taking her hand, "not always."

She leaned over and kissed him. As she did, her hair fell across his chest and face like a curtain of black silk.

If her hair was like silk, then her mouth and tongue were like velvet—hot velvet, searing his lips and the inside of his mouth.

She traced her nails across his chest and nipples, then moved her hand down to his pants, which she undid. He reached up and undid the buttons on her shirt. When he opened it, her breasts fell out into his hands, large and firm and on fire, like the rest of her.

If Armando chose *this* moment to sneak down, Clint would be extremely vulnerable.

•  •  •

It wasn't Armando who sneaked down while Clint and Delilah were involved with each other.

It was Julia.

She watched them for a few moments, then decided to go back to her wagon.

Delilah had gotten there first this time, but there would be another.

# FOUR

Delilah was astride Clint, his erection buried deep inside of her, her breasts dangling in his face so he could lick them and bite them while she rode him. They were both perspiring, the moonlight reflecting off their slick skin. Delilah's breath was coming in deep, shuddering breaths as she braced herself with her hands on his shoulders.

Clint's hands were on her back, pulling her toward him so he could lick every inch of her breasts, enjoying the salty taste of her.

She was a big woman, and he liked the way she felt heavy on him. When she brought her hips down on him, it jarred him, and the fact that they were on hard, unyielding ground made for the deepest penetration they could possibly hope for.

He saw her eyes widen and he knew she was going to come, so he allowed himself to explode at the same time. She moaned, bit her lip, then leaned all the way down so that she could bite *his*.

When the last vestiges of orgasm had faded from both of them, she stayed on him, tasting him again and again with her mouth on his, deep, noisy kisses, as if she couldn't get enough of him.

Finally she sat straight up on him, her hands still on his chest, and he looked up at her, at her proud, full breasts, at the way the moonlight reflected off her body, at the swollen mouth and heavy-lidded eyes. She leaned over and licked his chest once, taking a long, lingering taste of his salt, and then slid off him and onto the ground beside him.

Neither of them spoke. They both knew that what they had just experienced was beyond description, so neither of them tried to put it into words.

She stood up and walked into the stream and proceeded to wash herself. She bathed the sweat from her breasts and belly, her legs, washed her face and neck, and then washed herself between her legs. He watched with enjoyment as her muscles rippled and her breasts swayed before she moved back onto the bank near him.

He sat up, grabbed a blanket, and put it around her.

"You're going to catch cold."

"I like the cold breeze," she said. "It feels marvelous on my body."

It occurred to him then that he felt cold as well. He looked around for his clothes and pulled them on.

She used the blanket to dry herself and then also got dressed.

"I'd better get back to my wagon," she said.

"The one with Armando sleeping under it?"

She smiled and said, "Armando sleeps under Ivan's wagon, but I wouldn't want Julia to wake up and find me gone. She would know where I went."

"Would she tell anyone?"

"You mean Armando?" Delilah asked. "No, Julia wouldn't say anything. She would probably be sorry she didn't get here first."

"I don't know if I understand the relationship between all of you."

"I will explain another time."

"If there is another time."

She leaned over and kissed him deeply. She seemed to enjoy kissing very much, and she did it *very* well. She didn't seem to believe in small kisses.

"There will be another time," she said, her mouth still close to his. "There will be."

She left him then, walking away swiftly, as if she wanted to get away before she changed her mind.

Clint looked at the clear, cold water of the stream and shivered at the thought of bathing now. In the morning, when the sun was out, he would bathe. Now he was going to go to sleep, with the taste and scent of Delilah still on him.

Armando watched Delilah come from the direction of the stream back to her wagon. He knew she had been gone for hours because he had seen her go. He had also seen Julia leave her wagon and go that way, only to return.

After they went to Virginia City tomorrow and had their wheel fixed and returned Clint Adams's wheel to him, he would be glad to see Clint Adams go.

He did not want to have to fight the man for Delilah, for he knew that he would kill him, and they *did* owe him their gratitude for his assistance. It would not sit well with Ivan if he killed the man.

Then again, it would be different if *he* was king.

Julia heard Delilah come back to the wagon and pretended to be asleep. Delilah had been away for hours, and Julia could just imagine . . .

She heard Delilah give a sigh of contentment as she lay down to go to sleep.

Julia wanted Clint Adams more than ever.

# FIVE

Early the next morning eight riders stopped on a rise and looked down at the Gypsy wagons.

"See, Mr. Gordon? I told you they were there."

Gordon looked at Tom Mees, and then down at the Gypsy wagons.

"Gypsies," he said with distaste. "How long have they been there?"

"Since yesterday afternoon," Mees said. "They had a busted wheel."

"You think they're headed for Virginia City?"

"That's sure what it looks like to me," Mees said. He wasn't the foreman of Gordon's ranch, but he wanted to be. That was why he'd rushed to Gordon with this information when he first saw the wagons, and not to the foreman, Jack Weeks.

Gordon stared down at the wagons again, then looked at Mees.

"Take these men," he said, "and persuade them to go elsewhere."

Mees smiled and said, "I'll take care of it, Mr. Gordon. You can count on it."

"Just get it done," Gordon said. He wheeled his horse around and rode back to his ranch.

"You boys ready?" Mees asked.

"We're ready," one of the other men said, and the others nodded.

"Let's go shake up some Gypsies."


Delilah was up at the crack of dawn, a pleasant fatigue in her legs reminding her of the night before. She had just put on the coffeepot when she looked up and saw the men riding down on them.

She rushed to King Ivan's wagon and woke both Nicholas and Armando.

"What is it?" Armando asked.

"Riders," she said, "and they do not look friendly."

"Come," Armando said to Nicholas as both men scrambled from beneath the wagon.

"Delilah, into your wagon with Julia. Keep her there," Armando said.

Before she could obey, two things happened. Julia came out of the wagon, and the riders reached them.

"What do you want?" Armando called out.

There were eight men, and the one who was apparently the leader was a big blond man with a very insincere smile.

"We've come to give you a message, Gypsy," he said.

"What kind of message?"

Tom Mees didn't hear the question. He was looking at the two dark-haired women, as were the other men. During those moments Ivan and Maria stepped down from their wagon to see what was happening.

"What is it, Armando?" King Ivan asked. "What do they want?"

"Trouble, I think," Armando said.

Trouble he was afraid they might not be able to handle.


Clint was washing himself in the stream when he heard the shot. He paused to pick up his gun, and then ran for the wagons, clad only in his long underwear.

Mees dismounted and walked to Delilah, not because she was more to his liking but because she was closer.

"You Gypsy women are real pretty, aren't you?"

"Take your hands off her," Armando said, starting forward, but one of the mounted men pulled his gun and fired a shot at the ground at Armando's feet. None of the other men drew their guns. They didn't feel the need.

"Stand fast," Mees said. He still had hold of Delilah's arm.

"If you do not let go of her, he will have to kill me," Armando said, pointing to the man with the gun.

"Is that a fact?" Mees said. He looked at the man with the gun and said, "You heard the man, Jackson. Kill him!"

"Hold on, Mees!"

Mees turned and saw who had spoken. It was one of the other seven men, Dan Dundee. Dundee was the newest man on the ranch.

"What's your problem, Dundee?"

"Mr. Gordon said to run them off. He didn't say anything about killing them."

"Mr. Gordon told me to get the job done," Mees said, "so I'll get it done my way."

"I don't go in for any killing."

"Then my guess is that when we get back to the ranch, you'll be fired."

"There's no need for that," Dundee said. "I quit."

Dundee backed his horse up and separated himself from the rest of the group.

"Any of you other men have something to say?"

None of them spoke up.

"Good," Mees said. "Kill him, Jackson."

Jackson aimed his gun at Armando, who tensed, but before the man could fire, someone leapt from the second wagon. It was William, who had been hidden beneath the wagon where he slept. When he saw the men ride into the camp, he had hidden in the wagon.

He struck Jackson, causing the man to drop his gun, but William was so slight that he failed to knock Jackson from his saddle. Instead Jackson virtually caught the lad and flung him to the ground.

"William!" Julia shouted.

"Little bastard!" Jackson shouted. He pulled his rifle out of its scabbard and aimed at the boy, who was still struggling to get his wind back, unaware that he was seconds from death.

Clint came into view of the wagons in time to see young William flung to the ground. When the man aimed the rifle at the boy, Clint fired without thinking, taking the man from his saddle.

And then all the shooting started.

Armando shouted to Delilah, "Get under the wagon!"

Delilah raked Mees's face with her nails and pulled away from him.

Julia grabbed William under his arms and pulled him toward the wagon.

Ivan and Maria froze, but luckily the men were not shooting at her, they were shooting at Clint, who by now wished he had taken his rifle with him instead of his pistol.

He had to make every shot count, but even if he did, he was still a shot shy, unless he got some help.

Armando ran for Jackson's fallen gun and picked it up. He pointed it at the man nearest him and pulled the trigger. The bullet struck the man in the leg.

Dan Dundee fought to keep his horse under control, and when he did that, he pulled his gun. He had worked with these men for a few weeks, though, and couldn't bring himself to shoot any of them, so he simply fired in front of their horses, further spooking the already skittish animals.

Armando fired again, missing the man he was aiming at, but with him pulling the trigger, as well as Dundee and Clint, the men from Gordon's ranch decided it was time to retreat.

Mees ran for his horse, which pulled away from him, and then grabbed Jackson's horse and mounted up.

Clint fired again, striking another man in the chest, and then the men were riding away.

Dan Dundee didn't now quite what to do, so he rode away also, but instead of riding toward the ranch, he rode toward Virginia City.

Clint still had two shots in his gun, and there were

three dead men on the ground. Thanks to Armando picking up a gun, and one of their own men firing at the group, he hadn't had to empty his weapon.

Clint ran up to the wagons and said, "Is everyone all right?"

Armando looked at him, then turned and looked around him. Ivan and Maria were standing right where they had frozen, and miraculously they had not been hurt.

Armando looked frantically for Delilah, who was under her wagon with Julia and William.

"Are you all right?" he asked anxiously.

"Yes," Delilah said, "thanks to Clint."

Armando looked at Clint accusingly, then at the gun in his own hand. He made a face at it and dropped it.

"Is the boy all right?" Clint asked Armando.

Delilah came out from beneath the wagon and said, "William is all right. He just had the wind knocked out of him."

"He's a brave boy," Clint said. "He's the one you should be grateful to."

Julia came out from beneath the wagon, and after her came the boy, who was breathing normally again.

"Where's Nicholas?" Clint asked.

Everyone looked around then and saw Nicholas sitting on the ground with a bloody hole in his shoulder. No one had noticed before then that he had been wounded.

"Nicky!" Armando said, rushing to his younger brother's side.

"I'm all right," Nicholas said.

Clint crouched down by the big man and said, "Let me have a look."

Delilah was leaning over his shoulder as he examined the wound. There was no exit wound, so the bullet was still inside.

"Get some cloth and press it to the wound," Clint said to Delilah. "Bind it as tightly as you can."

"Yes, all right." And she hurried off for some cloth.

Clint said to Armando, "When he's patched up, get him in the wagon and head straight for Virginia City. I'll get dressed and meet you there to help you with the sheriff."

"We'll not talk to the sheriff," Armando said.

"Well, you may not, but I have to. I killed three men here."

"We didn't ask you to," Armando said.

"No, you didn't," Clint said. "I'll keep that in mind the next time I see one of you in danger of being killed."

# SIX

"What happened?" Sam Gordon demanded.

"They had a gunman with them," Tom Mees said. "He killed three of the men and wounded another."

"You came back with four."

"That was Dan Dundee," Mees said. "When the shooting started, he ran off."

"Coward!" Gordon said. "What were a bunch of Gypsies doing with a gunman?"

"I don't know, but he was good."

"Do you know who he was?"

"No idea."

Gordon studied Mees for a few moments, then said, "If you're lying to me, Mees—"

"I ain't lyin', Mr. Gordon, I swear."

"All right. Saddle my horse and Jack's."

"Jack?"

"We're going in to see the sheriff."

"Why do we need Weeks—"

"Just do as I say, Mees!"

"Yes, sir."

Gordon watched Mees leave his office and then sat down. Three men killed, all because of a bunch of Gypsies.

At first he was only going to have them run off. Now he was going to make them pay.

Clint got dressed, hooked up his team, and caught up to the Gypsy wagons just as they were entering Virginia City.

Riding behind the other two wagons, Clint was plainly able to see the looks of disgust the Gypsies were getting. He was also getting some looks, but they were looks of puzzlement. People were wondering if he was alone or with the Gypsies.

Virginia City's main street was wide enough for Clint to urge his team on and pull abreast of the first wagon, the one Nicholas was riding in.

"We'll stop at the doctor's first, and then go on to the livery," he told Armando.

"Where is the doctor's office?" Armando asked.

"I'll find out."

Clint rode ahead, then stopped his rig and asked someone, "Where's the doctor's office?"

"Up two blocks and around the corner to the right, mister," a man replied.

"Thanks."

"You hurt?"

"No."

"One of them?" the man asked, jerking his head toward the Gypsies.

"Yes, one of them."

"You a friend of theirs?"

Clint looked down at the man and said, "We're just acquaintances. Any more questions?"

The man looked away and said, "No, sir."

Clint waited for Armando to catch up to him.

"The doctor's office is two blocks up and around the corner to the right. You help him in there and we'll drop the wagons off at the livery and meet you there."

"All right," Armando agreed.

When they reached the corner, Clint got down and helped Armando get Nicholas out of the wagon.

"Can the king drive the wagon?" he asked.

"He will drive it."

"All right," he said. "We'll meet you in the doc's office. From there we'll go to the sheriff's office."

"*You* will go to the sheriff's office."

"Right," Clint said, "that's what I meant."


It was a day of arguments.

First Clint had to argue with the old liveryman, who didn't want to put up the three wagons. Finally he agreed to let them put them behind the barn and he would take care of the horses. The Gypsy wagons were being hauled by one horse each, while Clint's was pulled by a team of two—and then there was Duke. In the end it was the opportunity to take care of Duke that persuaded the liveryman.

"Do you have someone who can fix a busted wheel?"

"If it can be fixed."

"Well, have him look at it and let me know. If not, we'll have to buy a new one."

"All right."

"Uh, mister," the liveryman asked, "where are all these Gypsies gonna stay?"

"One thing at a time, mister," Clint said. "Please."

The second argument was with the doctor, who didn't want to treat Nicholas. Clint tried to reason with the man and talked about the Hippocratic oath.

Finally he said, "Either you treat him, or when I'm finished here, you'll need a new office."

The doctor stared into Clint's eyes and saw that he meant it.

"All right, I'll treat him."

"When you're finished," Clint said, "don't bother them for the money. I'll come back and pay you."

"Very well."

The third visit was to the sheriff's office, but when Clint walked in, he knew he was too late. There were three men there, and he recognized one of them as one of the men who had been at the Gypsy camp that morning.

"That's him," the man shouted as Clint entered. "That's the man."

The sheriff pulled his gun and trained it on Clint.

"You don't need that, Sheriff," Clint said. "I came on here on my own to clear this matter up."

"Just drop your gun," the sheriff said.

"Uh, not just yet," Clint said. "Not until I've had my say."

"I'm the law here, mister—"

"I know that, Sheriff," Clint said. "That's why I came here to speak to you. But tell me, are you *the* law or *his* law?"

Clint pointed to one of the other three men, the oldest one, who looked the most prosperous and therefore must have employed the other two. The man he recognized was sweating profusely. The other man, in his forties, heavy-lidded and dark, simply stared at Clint with interest.

"What's your name, mister?" the sheriff asked.

"Adams, Sheriff," Clint said. "Clint Adams. And your name?"

"I'm Sheriff Vincent Randle. Adams, Clint Adams? Is that what you said?"

"That's right."

The man licked his lips and said, "The Gunsmith?"

"I've been called that," Clint said. "You want to put that gun up? You don't need it, you know."

The sheriff hesitated, then probably realized that if the Gunsmith wanted to take him, his gun wouldn't help him any. He put it away.

"Have you heard this man's story?" Clint asked, indicating the sweaty man.

"He has."

"Fine," Clint said. "Now I'll tell you mine."

"This is preposterous!" the older man said.

He was in his fifties, very tall, barrel-chested and gray-haired.

"What's your name, sir?" Clint asked.

"I am Samuel Gordon. I own the S&G spread outside of town—the biggest ranch in the valley."

"I see, and these men work for you?"

"That's right."

"And the men who rode out to the Gypsy camp this morning, led by this man . . . they work for you?"

"That's right."

"Did you tell them to go out there, manhandle

women, and shoot a fourteen-year-old boy?"

"What?" Gordon said, looking at Mees.

"I didn't shoot no boy, Mr. Gordon," Mees said. "That was Jackson. He was gonna shoot the boy when . . ."

"When what?" Gordon asked.

"When I shot him," Clint said. "All this man did was harass the women."

Gordon turned, and as Mees was about to speak, the old man backhanded him across the face. Mees staggered back and only the sheriff's desk kept him from falling.

"You're fired, Mees."

"You can't fire me," Mees said, rubbing his cheek. "I was only doing what you told me."

"I told you to persuade them to bypass Virginia City," Gordon said. "I didn't tell you to kill them." Gordon looked at the other man and said, "Weeks, see that he's off my ranch today, and pay him off."

"Yes, sir."

The sheriff looked at Gordon and said, "Do you still want to press charges against the Gypsies, Mr. Gordon? Or against this—uh, Mr. Adams?"

"No," Gordon said, "I don't, Sheriff."

Gordon turned to Clint and said, "I don't condone manhandling women and killing children, Mr. Adams, but I do want those Gypsies out of Virginia City."

"Why is that, Mr. Gordon?" Clint asked.

"Well . . . because they're Gypsies!"

"Well, one of them was wounded by your men, and they have a broken wheel that has to be mended or replaced. They'll be here until all of that is taken care of."

"And I suppose you'll be their protector?"

"I don't know, Mr. Gordon," Clint said. "Will they need one?"

Gordon started for the door, then stopped and said, "I'll leave you to find that out for yourself, Adams."

# SEVEN

No amount of cajoling could get the hotel manager to give rooms to the Gypsies, and Clint didn't feel justified in threatening the man.

He went back to the livery and told the man there that the Gypsies would remain in their wagons, except for when the broken one was being fixed.

"Couldn't get them a hotel room, eh?"

"No," Clint said, "I couldn't."

"Well, tell 'em to stay back there, then," the man said.

"Thanks."

"Thank your horse," the liveryman said. "I've never had a beast like that in my stable before."

"Just treat him right."

"Oh, I will, you have no fear of that," the man said, "but I won't risk my business for your Gypsies."

"What does that mean?"

"That means that when the town decides it's time for them to leave, I don't want them back there anymore. Understood?"

"Understood."

Clint left the livery and went back to the doctor's office, where the Gypsies were waiting.

"Get these people out of my office!" the doctor shouted. "They've driving my patients away."

Clint looked at the doctor, a young man in his thirties who seemed immune to the charms of either Julia or Delilah. All he seemed to see when he looked at them was Gypsies.

"Have you finished with the wounded one? Nicholas?"

"Yes," the doctor said. "I took out the bullet and sewed him up. Get him out of here—out of town!"

"If he were a white man, what would you prescribe?"

"At least a week's rest—if he were a white man."

"Thanks, Doctor," Clint said. "What do I owe you?"

The doctor told him, and although Clint knew it was an inflated price, he paid it.

"Come on," he told the Gypsies, and they all followed him out of the office, Nicholas being supported by his brother.

He walked them back to the livery and Armando called out, "Why are we back here?"

Clint turned and told them, "I couldn't get you rooms at the hotel, so you'll have to stay in your wagons until Nicholas heals, and until the wheel is fixed or replaced."

"What about the sheriff?" Armando asked.

"I've already explained the situation to the sheriff," Clint said.

"He doesn't want to speak to us?" Delilah asked.

"No."

"And you are not under arrest?"

"Obviously not."

"You must be as good with your tongue as you are with your gun," she said.

He studied her face to see if she was playing with him or not.

"I'm going to get myself a hotel room and then a drink," he told them. "After that I'll bring you some food."

"That won't be necessary," Delilah said. "We can feed ourselves, but thank you, anyway."

"You're welcome."

Delilah turned and told Julia to take Ivan and Maria to their wagon. Armando had already walked Nicholas to the back.

"What do you want?" Delilah asked William.

"I want to go with *him*," the boy said, pointing at Clint.

"You have a conquest," Delilah said. "He thinks you are very brave."

"And I think he's very brave," Clint said, ruffling the boy's hair, bringing a smile from him, "but I can't take him into the saloon with me." He leaned over and said to the boy, "How about if I come back and get you, William, and take you to a restaurant to eat?"

William looked at Delilah and said, "Can I, Delilah? Can I?"

Delilah regarded Clint silently for a moment, then smiled at the boy.

"Yes," Delilah said, "you can."

"What about you?"

"Me?"

"Yes. Have lunch with us."

"I must feed the old ones."

"Can't Julia do that? And Armando?"

She studied him for a moment and then said, "Yes, I suppose they can. All right, William and I will both go to lunch with you."

"Good," he said. "I'll return for you after a few hours, when I've settled in and had a drink."

"We'll be ready, Clint."

He watched Delilah and William walk around behind the barn, then heaved a sigh of relief.

Now that the Gypsies were taken care of, he could see about getting himself settled in.

It had been an extremely eventful morning.

# EIGHT

When Clint walked into the saloon, he recognized a man standing at the bar. He had been one of the men who had ridden to the Gypsy camp that morning, the one who had *not* fired at him. When they had all ridden away, this man had ridden off on his own.

Clint walked over to the bar and stood next to the man.

"Beer," he said to the bartender.

The man gave him a brief glance, then went back to staring into his beer.

"You don't remember me, do you?" Clint asked when he had his beer.

The man looked at him.

"Should I?"

He appeared to be in his late twenties, tall and

slender, with brown hair that curled up around the base of his neck.

"We saw each other this morning," Clint said. "Of course, we were both dodging lead at the time."

The man studied him for a moment, then said, "Ah, the man in his long johns."

"That was me."

"Yeah, well, thanks to that little incident I'm out of a job."

"Seems to me that was your choice, wasn't it?"

"Yeah, I guess it was," the man said. "I just didn't hire on for any killing, especially not women and kids."

"Well, I appreciated your help."

"I wasn't shooting at anyone, you know."

"I know, but you added to the confusion, and that was a help."

Clint watched as the man emptied his beer mug and then said, "Can I buy you one?"

The man took a moment to think and then said, "Sure, why not?"

Clint ordered the beer and then said, "My name's Clint Adams, by the way."

"Adams," the man said. "The Gunsmith?"

Clint made a face and said, "Not my choice of names."

"What do you prefer?"

"Clint."

"All right, Clint," the man said. "My name is Dan Dundee."

"Mr. Dundee—"

"Dan."

"Drink up, Dan," Clint said.

Dundee sipped his fresh beer and then said, "You

know, if I had known who you were, I wouldn't have been so quick to help."

"Why not?"

"Well, you are the Gunsmith, aren't you? I mean, you could have handled them—"

"Your help was greatly appreciated, Dan," Clint said. "Remember, no matter what you think of me or my reputation, my gun only holds six shots, just like yours."

"Oh, that's right, isn't it?"

"Yes," Clint said, "it is."

Clint and Dan Dundee shared several beers and then Clint said, "Well, I have to go."

"So soon?"

"I have a lunch date with a lovely woman and a young boy."

"A woman?" Dundee asked. "One of the Gypsy women?"

"Yes."

"They were very beautiful, I noticed."

"Yes, they were."

"And it doesn't bother you that the woman you're seeing is a Gypsy?"

"No, it doesn't bother me, Dan. Would it bother you, with a woman that beautiful?"

"No, I guess it wouldn't," Dan said. "Not with a woman as beautiful as that young one. Is she the one?"

"The one?" Clint said, teasing him.

"The one you're having lunch with."

"Oh, no, I'm seeing the other one."

"Ah. She's beautiful too."

"Yes, she is."

"But the other one is so . . . so young. Her skin looked so . . . smooth . . ."

Three beers seemed to have affected Dundee much more than they had Clint. He wondered how many the younger man had had before he arrived at the saloon.

"Dan, it's kind of early to be drunk, don't you think?" Clint asked.

"Why? I don't have to go to work. I don't have a job."

"Do you have someplace to stay?"

"I have a hotel room."

"And money?"

"Enough to keep the room for a week or so."

"Do you know for a fact that you were fired?"

"Well, no . . ."

"Why don't you go to your hotel room, get some sleep, sober up, and then go and see Gordon. He wasn't too happy with what happened today. Maybe he won't fire you."

Dundee stared at Clint drunkenly for a moment, then said, "That's a real good idea. I'll go and see him right now."

"No, not now," Clint said. "Get some sleep, sober up, and then go see him."

Dundee stared at him some more and then said, "All right, that's what I'll do."

"Come on," Clint said, "I have to go to the livery, and the hotel's on the way. I'll walk you."

"You're a good friend, Clint," Dundee said, staggering to his feet, "a real good friend."

"Yep, that's me," Clint said, grabbing the man before he could fall down. "Everybody's good friend."

# NINE

Clint, Delilah, and William walked through town until they finally found a likely-looking restaurant. They went inside and were seated by a sour-looking waitress.

"What would you like, William?" Clint asked.

"I would love to have a steak and some potatoes, Clint."

"Then you'll have it. In fact, it sounds so good, I think I'll have the same."

Clint looked at Delilah, who said, "It sounds good to me too."

"Three steak dinners?" William said. "Oh, Clint, you must be rich."

"I'm far from rich, William, but I can afford three steak dinners."

Because of William's presence, Clint and Delilah did not talk about the things they wanted to talk about. In fact, William dominated most of the conversation, and Clint didn't mind. It had been a long time since he had talked with a child.

William wanted to know all about Clint, places he had been, things he had done. Clint did not once mention that he was called the Gunsmith. It wasn't something that he wanted the boy to key on.

After lunch he walked both Delilah and William around town before taking them back to the livery and to their wagons. Clint noticed the unfriendly and suspicious looks that Delilah and William were getting, and he also noticed some admiring looks she was getting from some of the men in town, but she and the boy didn't seem to notice any of it.

As William went running to the wagons to tell King Ivan and the others what he had eaten, Delilah turned to Clint to thank him.

"That's all right," Clint said. "It was my pleasure. He's a nice boy."

"*We* didn't get much time to talk, did we?" she said.

"Have dinner with me," he said. "We can talk then."

"All right."

"I'll go and check on that wheel for you."

"I will tell Armando."

"Until later, then," Clint said. She kissed his cheek and walked to the wagons.

Clint went into the livery to talk to the liveryman about the wheel.

"This is Buck," the liveryman said, indicating a bigger man wearing an apron. "He's the man who fixes the wheels, but he can't fix this one."

"Is that true?" Clint asked.

Buck nodded. He was a big man, standing about six-four, with huge forearms and a big belly that pushed at the front of the apron. It was big, but it was *hard*.

"Too much damage," Buck said. "Even if I patch it, it will crack at the first good bump. Look at it, it's been patched plenty of times before. They need themselves a new wheel."

Clint looked at the liveryman and said, "Will you sell them a new one?"

"Sure," the man said, pausing to spit a wad of tobacco juice onto the ground where Clint swore he saw it bounce. "But I got to send to Silver City for it."

"A big town like Virginia City and you don't stock wagon wheels?"

"I don't know if you know it, friend, but their wagons—and yours, too—are an odd size. It's a real coincidence that you happened to have one that fit, although if you look at it real close, yours is a little bigger than theirs."

Clint thought he had noticed something lopsided about the wagon while he was riding behind it into town but hadn't thought much about it at the time.

At that moment Armando came walking into the stable, and Clint told him the news.

"Impossible," Armando said.

"What is?"

"We do not have the money for a new wheel," he said. He looked at Buck and said, "Patch it."

"It ain't gonna hold up—"

"Patch it," Armando said, and turned and walked out.

Clint looked at the liveryman and said, "Order the new wheel."

"But if he can't pay for it—"

"Don't worry about that," Clint said. "I'll pay for the wheel. Just order it."

The liveryman shrugged and said to Buck, "Order it."

Clint left the stable and caught up to Armando before he reached the wagons. He grabbed the man's arm and spun him around.

"And you wonder why people don't like you?" he said. "Those men are willing to help you and you treat them like horse manure under your boot."

"They are doing nothing to help me. They will overcharge us, you watch."

"Maybe," Clint said, "but patching that wheel isn't going to get you very far before you get stuck again. If you patch it two or three times, you might as well buy a new one."

"I told you, we do not have the money."

"I'll pay for the wheel."

Armando gave Clint that suspicious look that was becoming very familiar.

"In return for what?" he asked.

"For God's sake, man, why do I always have to want to get something in return? I just want to help you and your people."

"Everyone wants something in return," Armando said. "We will leave when the wheel is fixed."

"What about Nicholas?"

"He will be fine—"

"If you make him travel, his wound is going to open," Clint said. "He needs to rest."

"They do not want us in this town."

"Maybe not, but at least here you won't be out on the road where you can be attacked by eight men. There's a sheriff in this town."

"He will not help us."

"Armando, talk to your people, see what they say—"

"*I* decide for my people."

"Oh, really? And when did you become King Armando?"

Armando gave Clint a long, hard look and then turned on his heels and stalked back to the wagons.

# TEN

After leaving Delilah, Clint went back to the sheriff's office to talk to Sheriff Randle.

"Mr. Adams!" Randle said when Clint walked in. The man jumped to his feet.

"Sit down, Sheriff," Clint said. "Relax."

"I hope you don't hold it against me what happened before, Mr. Adams," Randle said. "You gotta understand, Mr. Gordon's an important man around these parts, and I gotta live in this town."

"I understand, Sheriff," Clint said, "really I do. Now just relax, I just want to talk to you."

Randle sat down and visibly tried to relax.

"What can I do for you?"

"Well, for one thing, I'd like you to assure me that the Gypsies won't be bothered while they're in Virginia City."

51

"Well . . . how long will they be here for?" Randle asked nervously.

"Until the one who was shot heals, and until they can get a new wheel for their wagon."

"That could be a week or more."

"So?"

"I don't know if I can keep the lid on that long, Mr. Adams," Randle said. "I mean, Mr. Gordon just doesn't want them here, and although he wouldn't send his men to kill them, some of his men just might decide to do something on their own. Most of them are real loyal."

"I see," Clint said. "I see I'm going to have my hands full."

"W-what does that mean?"

"That means that anybody who goes after those Gypsies is going to have to go up against me—and you know what that means."

"Uh, n-no, no I don't," Randle said, his nervous condition worsening. "What does it mean?"

"It means there's going to be a lot of shooting, a lot of property damage, and maybe some innocent people getting hurt," Clint said. "The people of Virginia City are going to remember that come next election day."

"All right, look, Mr. Adams," Randle said. "I'll do what I can to keep people off them, but I'm only one man and I've got two deputies."

"A town this size should have half a dozen deputies," Clint said.

"Yeah, tell me about it. I've been short of deputies ever since I took office . . . but I'll do the best I can," Randle said.

"All right, Sheriff," Clint said, "you do the best you can and I'll do the best *I* can."

He started for the door, then stopped when he reached it and turned around.

"By the way, how do I get out to Mr. Gordon's ranch?" he asked.

"W-what are you going out there for?"

"I want to talk to the man," Clint said.

"Like you just talked to me?"

"Yeah, like I just talked to you."

Randle stood up, all jittery, and said, "That won't work, Mr. Adams. Gordon won't react to that. I mean, he *will* react, but not the way you want. He's a push-back kind of guy."

"I'm not going to push him, Sheriff," Clint said, "I'm just going to nudge him a little."

The sheriff started to shake his head, but Clint didn't give him time to speak.

"Can you keep the townspeople in line?"

"Well, they don't like Gypsies, but I think I can keep them out of trouble."

"Then you take care of the townspeople, and I'll take care of Gordon and his people."

"How?"

Clint scratched his nose and said, "I guess I'll have to think about that on the way out there. Now, how *do* I get out there?"

# ELEVEN

As Clint rode up to the Gordon house, a man was stepping down off the front steps. As he got closer, he recognized him as the man in the sheriff's office with Gordon. What was his name? Weeks, that was it.

As Clint approached the steps, the man moved forward to meet him. Recalling the conversation in the sheriff's office, Clint knew that Weeks was Gordon's foreman.

"Remember me?" Clint said.

"I remember you," Weeks said. "What do you want?"

"I want to talk to Mr. Gordon."

"He's not home right now."

"Where is he?"

"Out looking at some cattle."

"Well, just point me in the right direction and I'll find him."

"Why?"

"I want to talk to him."

"About what?"

"Gypsies," Clint said. "I understand it's a subject he's very interested in."

"When he gets back, I'll let him know you were here," Weeks said.

Clint was about to reply when he heard a horse approaching behind him. He turned to see if it was Gordon, but it was a woman—a girl, really, about the same age as Julia but blond.

"Jack," she said, "who's this?"

"He's just—"

"I'm looking for Mr. Gordon."

"Oh, well, I'm Lisa Gordon. Do you have business with my father, Mister . . ."

"Adams."

"Mr. Adams?"

"I do, Miss Gordon, but Mr. Weeks tells me he's out looking at some cattle."

"Yes, he's picking some out for a sale we're going to. Jack, I can take Mr. Adams out to Poppa."

"Lisa, I don't think that's—"

"That would be real nice, Miss Gordon," Clint said. "Thank you."

"Come on, then," she said. "Jack, I'll be back shortly."

She rode ahead of Clint, and he kicked Duke in the ribs and caught up to her in a few strides.

"That's a beautiful animal you're riding," she said.

"Thank you."

"You wouldn't consider selling him, would you?"

"No, I'm afraid not."

"I didn't think so," she said, "but I had to ask."

They rode a little farther and then she said, "What is the nature of your business with my father?"

"Ah, it's not exactly business that I have to talk to your father about," Clint said.

"If it's not business, then what is it? You're not a friend of my father's, are you?"

"No, we're not friends."

"You're being very mysterious, Mr. Adams."

"Please, call me Clint."

"And you can call me Lisa—if you'll tell me what you want to see my father about."

"Well, it has to do with Gypsies."

"Really? My father doesn't like Gypsies."

"Why not?"

"He says they're all thieves."

"And what do you say?"

"I don't know," she said, "I never met any."

"Has your father?"

"I don't know, Clint," Lisa said. "You'll have to ask him that."

"I intend to."

"What is it about Gypsies that you want to talk to him about?"

"Well, there are some Gypsies in town, and they've had a tough time lately. One of them got shot and they have a busted wagon wheel."

"What has that got to do with my father?"

"It's going to take some time for them to heal and get a new wheel, and I just want them to have that time. Your father has already said that he wants them out of town. I'd just like him to give them the time they need without putting any pressure on them."

"I see."

"Is your father that reasonable?"

"My father can be *very* unreasonable at times, Clint," Lisa admitted. "I guess you'll just have to see what kind of mood he's in today."

"Well, maybe having you along will put him in a good mood," Clint said. "I know seeing you has improved *my* mood tremendously."

"Why, Clint Adams," Lisa said, smiling at him, "I do believe you're a charmer."

"Well, I don't know about that—"

"Oh, I do," Lisa said, "but it will take a lot more than charm to get your way with my father—or with me, for that matter."

"Like father like daughter, is that what you're telling me?"

"Not exactly," she said, "although I've been known to be very disagreeable at times."

"I find that difficult to believe."

"Well, if you're around Virginia City long enough, Clint, you may find out firsthand."

# TWELVE

They reached a point where Clint saw a large herd of cattle being tended by a bunch of men. He followed Lisa Gordon until she found her father and rode toward him.

Gordon saw his daughter and smiled with unrestrained pleasure, but when he saw who was with her, the smile simply vanished.

"Hello, Poppa," she said.

"Hello, honey," he replied. She rode up to him and gave him a kiss. "I brought Mr. Adams with me, Poppa, although to tell you the truth, I'm not sure I should have. I think maybe I did something without thinking it through again."

"That's all right, honey," he said. "Why don't you go back to the house. I'll speak to Mr. Adams."

"All right, Poppa," she said. She turned and

59

looked at Clint over her shoulder. All he could see were her huge blue eyes.

"Good luck, Clint."

"Thank you, Lisa."

"Bye, Daddy," she said, and headed back to the ranch.

"Where the hell did you meet my daughter?" Gordon exploded when Lisa was out of earshot.

"Just a little while ago, at your house."

"And you're on a first-name basis with her?"

Clint shrugged.

"Friendly people get on a first-name basis fairly quickly, Gordon."

The older man pointed his finger at Clint and said, "Well, you'd better get *un*friendly with my daughter real quick, Adams."

"Look, Gordon," Clint said, "I didn't come out here to argue with you about your daughter."

"No, you came out to talk about those damn Gypsies of yours."

"What have you got against Gypsies?"

"Everybody knows they're a bunch of thieves," Gordon said. "If we let them stay around, they'll steal us blind and pollute our land."

"Pollute the land? With what?"

Gordon pinned him with a hard stare and said, "Magic!"

"What the hell are you talking about?"

"Black magic," Gordon said, "and don't tell me you don't know about Gypsies and their magic."

"Look, Gordon, I came out here to ask you for some time for the Gypsies. They're waiting for a new wheel—"

"Get those people out of Virginia City as soon as

possible, Adams," Gordon said. "That's all I'm gonna tell you. Get them out before something ugly happens."

Clint stared at Gordon and then said, "You have to be the most narrow-minded, disagreeable . . . How you ever fathered a daughter as sweet as Lisa—"

"Don't you talk about my daughter, Adams, and don't you try to see her, either," Gordon said, spittle wetting his chin. "Reputation or no reputation, you're gonna find yourself dead!"

Clint waited a beat and then said, "There's no need for threats like that, Gordon. You're turning this into something that there is absolutely no call for. You'd better do some heavy thinking about the things you've been saying. I'll be in Virginia City for a while, and so will the Gypsies. When you want to talk some sense, you come and see me."

"The only time I'll come and see you is if you try to see my daughter again."

"All I did was ride out here with her," Clint said. "Don't make mountains where there aren't any."

"Get off my land, Adams, before I call some of my men over."

"You do that," Clint said, feeling silly himself for posturing, "and you're going to have to hire yourself a lot more men."

As Clint rode away from Sam Gordon, Lisa Gordon watched from a distance. She had not ridden back to the ranch, she had only ridden off a hundred yards or so to watch the conversation between her father and Clint Adams.

She found Clint Adams to be an extremely attractive, very interesting man. It had been plain to her

that her father was angry and had been shouting at
Adams, and the other man had not backed down at
all.

Lisa had never met a man who was not afraid of
her father.

Maybe today she had, and now she wanted to get
to know him better.

She decided to follow him part of the way back to
Virginia City.

Clint knew somebody was trailing him, but he
didn't know who. He wondered if Gordon had been
angry enough to send a man after him to bushwhack
him.

He stuck to the main road back to Virginia City
because he knew there was a sharp bend in the road
near a stand of cypress trees. When he reached the
sharp bend, he guided Duke behind the stand of trees
and waited to see who was tailing him. He was surprised when he saw Lisa Gordon come around the
corner.

"Lisa."

He rode out from the trees and she stopped her
horse and looked behind her.

"You frightened me."

"What are you doing on my trail, Lisa? I thought
you went back to the ranch."

"I've never met a man who wasn't afraid of my
father, Clint," she said. "You aren't afraid of him,
are you?"

"No."

"You see? I just wanted to learn more about you."

"By following me?"

"For a start."

"I don't think this is such a good idea, Lisa."

"Why not?" she said. "Don't you find me attractive?"

"I find you very attractive, Lisa."

She had a beautiful face and a taut body. Her breasts were small, but he could see that they were very firm. How could he *not* find her attractive? She had a mouth that looked as if it would burst with sweet juices if he bit into it.

"Then what's the problem?" she asked.

"Your father and I are ... making faces at each other."

"What?"

"We're like two bull elks, posturing and posing at each other before we lock antlers."

"I don't think I understand this, Clint," she said. "I thought you weren't afraid of my father."

"I'm not," Clint said, "but that doesn't mean I'm looking to lock antlers with him."

"And if we see each other, you will?"

"To tell you the truth we may, anyway, whether you and I see each other or not, but if we do see each other, I don't want you to think it's because I'm trying to get under his skin."

"Would that be the reason?"

"No."

"I believe you," she said. "See, now we can get to know each other better."

"Lisa," he said, "let's put this aside for the moment. I have to get back to town."

"Oh, I didn't mean right here and now," she said, smiling at him, "but soon."

"How soon?" he asked. He was sure that he had

the suspicious look on his face that he had gotten used to seeing on Armando's face.

"Soon enough," she said. "I'll let you know when."

"You're not going to follow me back to town now, are you?"

"No," she said, "I'm going home now, but keep looking over your shoulder, Clint Adams." She smiled at him and said, "You'll never know when I'll be there."

# THIRTEEN

Clint got back to town in time to bathe and pick up Delilah for dinner. She was very quiet as they walked to the hotel, where he intended to buy her dinner in the dining room.

They were seated gingerly, by a waiter who seemed to think that something might rub off if Delilah got too close to him.

"Is something wrong?" he asked her.

"No," she said, and then, "Yes."

"What?"

"Armando."

"What did he do?"

"He's pressuring King Ivan."

"To do what?"

"Leave."

"Despite Nicholas's condition?"

"Yes," Delilah said. "He wants to get away from you."

"What about the wheel?" he asked. "You have to wait for the wheel."

"He insists that the wheel can be repaired, and that we won't have to wait for a new one."

"Well, that's true," Clint said, "but a patched wheel won't last very long. You could get five miles out of town and be back in the same predicament."

"That is what I said, but Ivan has always listened to Armando."

"And is he this time?"

"He hasn't said yet," Delilah said. "He will probably decide tomorrow."

"Well, then, we have tonight," Clint said. "Let's make the most of it."

She stared at him and said, "Well, I guess this is more than I expected to have. I thought there would only be that night by the stream."

"Will you marry Armando, eventually?"

"I don't know."

"You never did explain your relationship with him."

"Well, Julia and William are Ivan and Maria's grandchildren. My mother was King Ivan's brother. She died when I was born, and I was brought up by her cousin."

"Wait," Clint said, "I think I'm confused. You are related, aren't you?"

"Yes, we are, we're cousins . . . by marriage. We were brought up almost as brother and sister."

"But he loves you?"

"Yes," she said. "He thinks we should marry."

"And who makes the final decision?"

"Ivan."

"Not you?"

"We just do whatever the king says."

"That doesn't sound like much of a life."

"It is my life."

"I'm sorry, I didn't mean to offend—"

"No, no," she said, covering his hand with hers, "you didn't offend me. I know our ways must seem strange to you, but your ways—the ways of the *gajo* —are strange to us too."

"*Gajo*?" he repeated.

She smiled and said, "It is our word for those who are not Romany, Gypsies."

Clint had been to San Francisco many times, to Chinatown, and he knew that the Chinese had a word for the whites, *lo fan*. He imagined that *gajo* must have been much the same thing.

"Well," Clint said, "how would you like this *gajo* to order dinner for you?"

"I would like that very much."

After dinner they went for a walk through town, as they had that afternoon, only this time they didn't have young William chattering in their ear.

"William seems to look to you for guidance," Clint said.

"I guess he sees me as a mother figure," Delilah said. "Maria is really too old to fill that position, and Julia is his sister and only five years older."

"I see. Well, you seem to have done well with him so far. He was certainly brave enough this morning."

"Was it only this morning?" she asked. "It seems like something that happened so long ago."

"I know."

"William is more headstrong than brave, Clint,"

Delilah said. "I wish he could be around you more and learn the difference."

"Well, if you don't leave tomorrow..."

"Yes," she said, squeezing his hand. "If..."

"Could we go back now?" she asked after a few moments.

"To the wagons?"

"No," she said, looking up at him, "to your hotel room."

He put his arm around her waist and said, "I think that can be arranged."

When they got to his room, she turned and moved into his arms right away. They kissed, a long, deep kiss, and during it they proceeded to undress each other. When they were naked, they sank down onto the bed together and his lips began an odyssey of her body. He tasted every inch of her while she moaned and writhed beneath him, and then he nestled his face between her legs and drove her into a frenzy.

"Oh, please, Clint..." she moaned. "Now... now... please..."

He moved over her and entered her in one swift movement that drove the breath from her. He paused a moment, letting her take a deep breath, and then began to move inside of her, sliding his hands beneath her to cup her buttocks and gather her to him.

"Oh, yes..." Delilah moaned. "Yes..." raking his back with her nails, drumming his buttocks with her heels.

She kissed him deeply and muttered against his mouth, "We have tonight, we have... all... night."

Julia Miro watched as Clint and Delilah went into his hotel. She had been hoping that Clint would sim-

ply walk Delilah back to the wagons and go to his
room alone, after which she would join him. Now
she knew that was not going to happen. Delilah had
beaten her to Clint again, and it was possible that
they might leave tomorrow.

Julia knew that barging in on them would accom-
plish nothing. She decided to be very adult about the
whole thing and go back to the wagons.

If they did *not* leave tomorrow, she would have
another chance.

# FOURTEEN

Early the next morning Delilah woke up and slipped from the bed.

"Where are you going?" Clint asked.

She leaned over and kissed him deeply, her tongue intertwining with his.

"I have to go," she said, standing up and starting to dress. "This morning Ivan will make up his mind about whether we are to leave or stay. I have to be there to try to dissuade him."

He watched with pleasure while she dressed.

"If they move Nicholas, it will not be good for him," she said, "and we need that new wheel."

Clint remained silent while she talked and dressed and just watched her.

When she was dressed, she leaned over and kissed him again, as if she were trying to devour him. He'd

71

never known a woman who enjoyed kissing as much as she did.

"Of course," she said, "those aren't the only reasons I don't want to leave."

He smiled and said, "I didn't think that they were."

Clint was going to have breakfast and then remembered his wheel. If Armando *was* going to have the wheel patched, then Clint was going to have to get his wheel back. Then he remembered that he had given the liveryman the go-ahead to order a new wheel. If the Gypsies left town, he was going to be stuck waiting for the new wheel—and paying for it.

Then he got an idea. He could sell the Gypsies *his* wheel, the one that was already on their wagon, and then wait for the new one and keep that as his spare. At least that would get the Gypsies on their way with a sound wheel and they'd get a little farther then five miles, when the patched wheel would invariably break down again.

He walked toward the livery, with intentions of doing what he could to see that the Gypsies got safely on their way—if that was what they really wanted to do.

"Why are we gonna do this?" Del Crandall asked.

Jay McCain, Lucas Mann, and Ted Gold all stared at Crandall.

"We've told you this before, Del," McCain said. "These are Gypsies. If they're allowed to stay in town, they'll steal from all of us."

"Also, Mr. Gordon wants them gone," Mann said.

"It wouldn't hurt us to have an important man like Sam Gordon owing us a favor."

"And did you get a look at their women?" Gold asked. "Their hair is so dark and their skin is so smooth."

"I noticed," McCain said.

"Are we doing this?" Gold asked.

"We're doing it," McCain said, "for the good of the town."


Clint entered the livery stable and saw the livery-man sitting in a chair with his eyes closed. For a moment he thought the man was dead, but then he saw his chest rising and falling.

As Clint approached, the man opened his eyes.

"The wheel will be here in two days," he said.

"That's good."

"I guess you're here about the trouble?"

"What trouble?"

"I guess you're not here about the trouble."

"*What* trouble?"

"The trouble your friends the Gypsies are having," the livery man said. "I just saw two of Sam Gordon's men go back there a few moments ago with two of the town toughs."

"You mean the Gypsies?"

"Yes, the Gypsies."

Clint started out the front door, and the liveryman said, "You could go out on the side and come up on their blind side."

Clint looked at the man, then said, "Thanks," and went to the side door.

He moved around the livery stable to the back, and when he came within sight of the wagons, the four white men couldn't see him, but Delilah and Julia and William could. Nicholas was probably still in the wagon, as were Ivan and Maria. Armando, owever, was on the ground and was bleeding from the head. One of the white men had his gun out and apparently had pistol-whipped Armando.

"Now," the man with the gun was saying, "we'll take your women with us for a few hours of fun, and when we bring them back, you will be ready to leave."

"You will have to kill me first," Armando said from the ground, "before I let you take them."

The man with the gun laughed and looked at his friends, then said, "That could be arranged, Gypsy."

The man raised the gun again, intending to hit Armando with it a second time.

"I'd advise you to leave that hand up there," Clint called out.

The white men turned and stared at Clint.

"What are you, a Gypsy lover?" the man with the gun said.

"These people are friends of mine," Clint said. "If you're going to cause them trouble, I am going to cause you trouble."

The man laughed.

"You think you can?" he said. "Against the four of us?"

"Your friends look smarter than you," Clint said. "I don't think they want to die. Do you?"

The man with the gun looked uncertain for a moment. His hand was still up in the air, holding the gun.

"Put your gun back in your holster," Clint instructed.

The man kept staring at Clint, trying to decide what he should do.

"Do it," Clint said. "You three men, back away. I want you to watch what happens between your friend and me, and then you can decide if *you* want to try your hand."

The man with the gun lowered his hand slowly and slid his gun back into his holster.

"What's your name?" Clint asked him.

"McCain."

"All right, McCain, any time you're ready."

"McCain," one of the other men said, "that's gotta be the man who killed three of Gordon's men yesterday. His name's Adams, McCain, Clint Adams." And then, as if McCain didn't know what that meant, the other man said, "The Gunsmith, McCain!"

"Quiet down," Clint said. "Let Mr. McCain make up his own mind."

"Now wait a minute," McCain said. "Look, we were only trying to have some fun—"

"At the expense of peace-loving people, right? These people aren't bothering anyone, and I expect the same from the people of this town. Which of you are from town?"

Two of the men raised their hands.

Clint looked at McCain and said, "That means you work for Gordon."

"Th-that's right."

"And you?" Clint said, looking at the fourth man.

"That's right."

"What's your name?"

"Mann."

"Well, McCain and Mann, you go back and tell

your boss that he'll be receiving a medical bill for
this little visit. You other two, go over and talk to the
sheriff."

"What?" one of them asked.

"I'll check with the sheriff later. If you haven't
been to see him, I'll come looking for you."

The four men exchanged glances.

"Now move!" Clint said.

The four men walked away slowly, looking behind them to be sure Clint wasn't going to shoot
them in the back.

Clint walked over to Armando and assisted Delilah in helping him to his feet.

Armando pulled his arm away from Clint and
said, "I do not need your help."

He staggered over to the wagon, which he used to
keep upright.

"Delilah, take him over to the doctor and have
him patched up. I guess you won't be leaving today."

"No," she said. "We did not even get a chance to
discuss it with Ivan this morning."

"Well, the new wheel will be here in two days,"
Clint said. "It's probably best that you wait at least
until then."

"I agree," she said, "and I will tell Ivan."

"Take Armando over to the doc now."

"Yes," she said. "Julia, help me."

"Yes, Delilah."

Julia gave Clint a long look before going to help
Armando.

William came over to Clint and looked up at him
adoringly.

"Would you really have killed all four of them?"

"William, do you think any one man can kill four others just like that?"

"You could."

"Young man," he said, "you and I will have a talk later. Right now you go and check on Nicholas."

"All right," William said. He started to run to the wagon, then turned and called back, "You were wonderful!" before continuing on.

# FIFTEEN

"You fools!"

Jay McCain flinched as Sam Gordon shouted at him and Lucas Mann.

"We were just trying to do you a favor, Mr. Gordon," McCain said.

"Yeah, Mr. Gordon," Mann said. "McCain said you'd appreciate it."

"Shut up, Mann!" McCain said.

"Why do I have so many morons working for me?" Gordon lamented. "Get out, both of you!"

"Uh, are we fired, Mr. Gordon?" McCain asked.

"I'll let you know when you're fired. Just get out of my office."

McCain and Mann hurried to the door to get out while they still had a job, and on the way out they passed Lisa Gordon.

"What's the matter, Poppa?" she asked. "I could hear you shouting outside."

"I have idiots working for me, that's what's the matter," Gordon said.

"You hired them, didn't you?"

"No," Gordon said, "I didn't, Jack Weeks did. Lisa, honey, could you get Jack in here for me?"

"I'll get him, Daddy, but you have to promise me you won't yell so much. It's not good for you."

Sam Gordon took a deep breath and said, "All right, honey, I'll try."

As Lisa left the office, Sam Gordon sat down and thought about how much he loved his daughter. Everything he was building he was building for her, and he wasn't going to let a bunch of Gypsies ruin it for her.

Not even if it meant tangling with the Gunsmith.

Clint stopped at the doctor's office to make sure the doctor knew who was paying Armando's medical bill. After convincing the man that the only way he was going to get his money was from Sam Gordon, Clint went to the sheriff's office.

"Oh, not again," Randle said, standing up.

"Don't get so nervous every time I show up here, Sheriff," Clint said. "Did two men come by?"

"Yeah, they did," Randle said. "Ted Gold and Del Crandall. What did you send them here for?"

"Didn't they tell you?"

"They said you sent them over because two of Gordon's men were bothering the Gypsies."

"They didn't say that they were there also?"

"They said they were passing by and you thought they were there."

"And what did you do?"

"I fined them ten dollars each for wasting my time," Randle said. "Why, what did you want me to do?"

"That'll do, Sheriff," Clint said, "that'll do."

"What about Gordon's men?"

"A couple of boys named McCain and Mann. I sent them back to their boss with a message."

"Did you, uh, see Mr. Gordon yesterday?"

"Yes, I did, and we didn't exactly have a friendly conversation."

"I knew it," Randle said. "These Gypsies are gonna knock the roof right off this town."

"Look, Sheriff," Clint said, "another one of those Gypsies was injured by another one of Gordon's men. Now, if it wasn't for the fact that the Gypsies don't trust the law, they'd be pressing charges right now."

"Adams, I can't be arresting Gordon's men—"

"You might not have to," Clint said, walking to the door. "You might just end up burying them."

Clint went from the sheriff's office to the saloon and found Dan Dundee there, standing in the same place he'd been standing in the day before.

"Hello, Dan," Clint said.

Dundee looked at Clint and said, "Where have you been?"

"Around. Beer," Clint told the bartender.

"How are your Gypsies doing?"

"Not real well," Clint said. "It's a full-time job making sure no one bothers them." He told Dundee what Gordon's men had done to Armando that morning.

"Gordon's a tough man, Clint," Dundee said.

"Speaking of Gordon, did you talk to him about your job?"

"Naw," Dundee said, "I decided I don't *want* to work for him."

"What about pay owed you?"

"It's only one day, and I ain't gonna go out there and ask for it."

Clint sipped his beer, mulling over an idea that just came to him. He wasn't sure if he should approach Dundee with it or not, then decided to go ahead.

"How would you like to work with me?"

"Doing what?" Dundee asked.

"Keeping an eye on the Gypsies."

"You mean, go against Gordon and his men?"

"Not necessarily. There might not be any more incidents."

"And then again, there might," Dundee said. "I don't know. . ."

"Think about it," Clint said. "I can't pay you much."

"Why would you pay me at all?" Dundee asked, looking puzzled. "I mean, what's it to you if a bunch of Gypsies get run out of town?"

"I like them, Dan," Clint said, and then added, "Some of them, anyway."

"The women?"

"And the boy," Clint said. "Hell, I like most of them, and I don't like seeing people pushed around."

"And you're willing to spend money to see that it doesn't happen?"

Clint shrugged.

"What else is money for?"

"I don't know," Dundee said. "I've never had enough to worry about it."

"Well," Clint said, putting his empty mug down, "let me know if you change your mind. I don't relish standing off a whole town alone."

"Whereas two of us would make a big difference," Dundee said sarcastically.

"You never know, Dan," Clint said, slapping the man on the back. "See you later."

Clint Adams left and Dan Dundee thought over his offer with another beer. Dundee had never made a habit of dealing himself into another man's game, not even when he was invited.

He wasn't sure he wanted to take a hand in this one.

# SIXTEEN

"Jack?"

Jack Weeks looked up, not at the sound of his name but at the sound of Lisa Gordon's voice. For the past year Weeks had been falling more and more in love with Lisa, even though she was only nineteen and he was almost twenty years older. He'd first noticed her—really noticed her as a woman—when she turned sixteen, but he'd been able to force himself to continue thinking of her as a child, until last year, when she turned eighteen.

"Hello, Lisa."

"Poppa wants to see you, Jack."

"Do you know what about?"

"No, I don't," she said, "but I can probably guess."

So could Weeks.

"All right, honey," he said, "I'll go and see him."

85

"Jack?"

"Yes?"

"I've asked you to stop calling me honey. Could you do that for me?"

"Lisa, you know how I feel—"

"Jack, please!"

"All right," he said. "All right, Lisa, whatever you want."

"You had better go and see Poppa."

"Yeah," he said, and walked away.

Lisa watched Jack Weeks go into the house and wondered if she should talk to her father about him. More and more she was bothered by the way Weeks looked at her, talked to her, even *touched* her, but she didn't want to get him fired.

That is, unless she had to.

Weeks entered Gordon's office and waited for the older man to speak to him.

"Weeks," Gordon finally said, "how many morons have you hired?"

Weeks knew exactly what he was getting at, and he didn't back down.

"Mr. Gordon, you gave me the power to hire and fire, and I hire the men I think can do the job. I don't hire them for their brains, I hire them for their ability to take orders and to do the job."

"All right, all right," Gordon said, "you have a point."

"Thank you."

"I want you to make sure the *morons* stay away from those Gypsies," Gordon ordered. "Make damn sure they understand this!"

"Yes, sir. Anything else, sir?"

"Yes," Gordon said. "I want you to get your best men together, the ones that have a few brains and know enough to follow orders."

Weeks asked the next question, even though he had a good idea of what the answer was going to be. He hadn't worked for Sam Gordon for ten years— five as foreman—without learning to read the old man's mind.

"Yes, sir," Weeks said, "and what do you want me to do with them?"

Gordon stood up and said, "I want you to get those goddamn Gypsies out of Virginia City and as far from my land as possible. Do you think you can take care of that, Weeks?"

"I think so, sir," Weeks said, "as long as you don't care how."

"I don't want any rapes or unnecessary killings!" Gordon said. "I hope I make myself clear on that. Just get the job done."

"Yes, sir, no unnecessary rapes or killings."

Jack Weeks withdrew from the room.

Unnecessary, he thought, was in the eyes of the beholder.

# SEVENTEEN

"You did a good job," the liveryman said to Clint as Clint passed his door.

"What?"

"Of avoiding trouble this morning," the man said, "you did a good job."

"Are you looking for an excuse to make them leave too?" Clint asked.

"Hell no. They ain't botherin' me none."

"What's your name, old-timer?"

"Winder."

"That's all?"

"That's what they call me."

"Well, Winder, I don't suppose you'd like to help me keep on avoiding trouble, would you?"

"Nope," the old man said. "I don't mix in other folks' business."

"That's a good practice," Clint said. "I wish I could do the same."

"One of them busybodies, huh?"

"Yep," Clint said, "I'm one of them busybodies."

Clint waved at the old man and walked back to where the Gypsy wagons were. Julia was hunched over a fire, and Delilah was stepping down from one of the wagons.

"Hello," Julia said, standing up.

"Hello, Julia."

"I haven't seen much of you lately," she said, her hands clasped behind her back. In her own way she was as lovely as Lisa Gordon. They both had that youthful glow to their skin, although Julia was dark and Lisa was pale. If it wasn't for Delilah, he'd be in a quandary about which one to chase—or he'd be tempted to try to juggle both of them at the same time.

*Maybe, I'm getting too old for that, though,* he thought.

"Hello, Clint," Delilah said. "Julia, Armando needs some of that soup."

"I'll take it to him," Julia said.

They waited for Julia to go into the wagon before speaking.

"How's Armando?"

"Dizzy," Delilah said, "and he has a headache. The doctor said he'd have both for a while."

"Have you spoken to Ivan?"

"Yes. He's agreed that we should at least stay until the new wheel comes."

"That's good. Can you leave for lunch?"

"I don't think so," she said. "I want to stay near for Nicholas and Armando, as well as the old ones."

"Where's William?"

"In the wagon with Armando and Nicholas."

"Think he'd want to have lunch with me?"

"I'm sure he would."

As Delilah was walking to the wagon Clint got an idea and called out, "Ask Julia also."

Delilah turned and came back.

"Is that a good idea?"

"Trust me," Clint said. "I have a young man I want her to meet."

Delilah studied him a moment, then said, "All right, I'll trust you."

"Will you be able to have dinner with me later?" he asked, touching her face.

"I will make sure I have the time," she said. She closed her eyes and leaned into his touch for a moment, then turned and went to the wagon.

William was only too happy to have lunch with Clint, as was Julia.

"Can we go to the same place and have steak again?" he asked.

"If Julia doesn't mind," Clint said.

"I don't mind at all," Julia said, hanging on to his left arm happily.

As they went past the saloon Clint stopped and said, "Wait a minute. There's a friend of mine in here who I'd like to invite to lunch. Wait out here."

He stepped inside the saloon and saw Dundee still standing at the bar.

"Hey, Dundee!"

Dundee turned and grinned when he saw Clint.

"Come on, we're going for lunch."

"Who's we?" Dundee asked.

"Come on out and see."

Dundee shrugged and turned away from the bar. Clint went outside, and when Dundee came out and saw Julia, his eyes lit up. Clint thought he saw a hint of interest in Julia's eyes as well.

"Dan Dundee, this is Julia and her brother, William," Clint introduced.

"I'm real pleased to meet you," Dundee said, staring at Julia, and then he looked at William and added, "Both of you."

"We're going to the café for steak," Clint said. "You interested?"

"Oh," Dundee said, looking at Clint, "I'm interested."

# EIGHTEEN

Lunch went fine.

Clint was able to sit back and let the others carry the conversation. He was pleased to see that Dan Dundee and Julia were getting on very well.

William was sitting next to Clint, and Dundee and Julia were sitting side by side. Clint tried to answer all of William's questions while keeping an eye on Dundee and Julia.

After lunch, outside the café, Clint asked William if he wanted some candy.

"Oh, I would very much like some candy."

"Dan," Clint said, "I'm going to buy William some candy. Why don't you walk Julia back to the wagons?"

"If she doesn't mind," Dundee said, "I'd be happy to."

"I do not mind," she said. She turned to Clint and

said, "Thank you very much for lunch."

"It was my pleasure, Julia."

He watched Dundee and Julia walk off and noticed that Julia was hanging on to Dan's arm the way she had been hanging on to *his* arm a little while ago.

"Are we going for candy now?" William asked.

"Yes, William," Clint said, "we are going for candy now."

Clint brought William back to the wagons and then returned to the hotel, where he found Dan Dundee waiting for him in the lobby.

"All right, you win," Dundee said.

"What does that mean?"

"It means I'll help you keep the Gypsies out of trouble."

"What made you change your mind?"

"As if you didn't know," Dundee said. "That was a sneaky trick, introducing me to them like that."

"Maybe," Clint said, "but it worked, didn't it?"

"Yep," Dundee said, "it sure did."

Clint and Dundee made their plans over drinks at the saloon.

"One of us will have to be with them at all times," Clint said, "but you have to understand, Armando won't want either one of us there."

"Well, as long as he's inside one of the wagons with dizziness and a headache, he won't know, will he?"

"Maybe none of them should know you're there, Dan," Clint said. "Maybe you should keep a discreet distance from the wagons, out of sight."

"I could stay inside the livery," Dan said, "but now that you've introduced me to Julia, don't expect me to keep my distance from her."

"No, I wouldn't expect that."

"How should we break up the shifts?"

"I don't know," Clint said. "I want to be free to move around, to talk to Gordon if I have to, or to the sheriff."

"All right, then," Dundee said, "you'll relieve me when you can. I'll try to bear up under the burden of watching Julia all day."

"That's real big of you, Dan," Clint said, "real big."

After Jack Weeks had gone in to see her father, Lisa Gordon decided to go for a ride. She saddled her mare, and before long she was on her way to town, even though that had not been her original intention.

It was time to pay a surprise visit on Clint Adams.

Clint left Dan Dundee at the livery, already standing his first shift. The liveryman, Winder, didn't seem to mind, especially when Clint gave him a little extra money.

Clint decided to go back to his room, for want of something better to do. He felt like he had been on the go for two days without much rest.

Maybe that was what he needed, a little rest.

As Clint approached the door to his room he saw a shadow move beneath it, signaling that there was someone inside. He drew his gun, turned the doorknob slowly, and then slammed the door open.

The girl on the bed jumped, dropping the sheet so that he could see that she was completely naked. He had been right about her breasts. Though small, they were extremely firm and seemed to jut from her chest.

"Lisa . . ."

"You seem to be making a habit out of frightening me," she said.

"Lisa . . ."

She got up on her knees and extended her arms to him.

"Now you're just going to have to calm me down."

# NINETEEN

"Lisa . . ."

"You keep saying my name," Lisa said. "Aren't you glad to see me?"

"That's a difficult question to answer."

She smiled because she could see the way he was looking at her—all of her.

"I see you *are* attracted to me, after all."

"I told you I was."

"Come here."

He approached the bed and she moved to the edge of it, still on her knees. He could feel the heat her body was giving off.

As he came near she reached out and touched his crotch. Beyond his control, he had swelled with desire, and she was able to feel him.

"Yes," she said, "you do find me attractive."

She undid his gun belt and let it drop to the floor.

She started on his pants and he grabbed her hands.

"Lisa, listen—"

"If you reject me," she said, "I'll be very angry. I might even scream."

"Look—"

"Then my father would find out about this, and I really couldn't admit that I had come here on my own."

"That's blackmail."

She laughed and said, "I know."

She reached for his neck and pulled his face down to hers. Her hot mouth covered him with kisses and then fastened onto his. As he had imagined, her lips felt like ripe fruit, and her kisses were juicy and sweet.

What the hell, he thought.

She had the firmest breasts he had ever encountered.

He found himself entranced by them, by the way they felt beneath his lips, by the way her nipples reacted to his tongue.

"Oh, God, yes..." she moaned as he sucked her breasts, and then he felt her shudder with orgasm and knew she was an extremely sensous, sensitive girl. Her sexual reactions to the slightest stimuli were extreme.

He slid one finger into the steaming depths of her, and she shuddered again, gasping for breath. He thumbed her clit and she cried out, her whole body trembling.

He couldn't wait any longer. He wanted to see how she reacted when he entered her.

He mounted her and pressed the head of his cock up against her moist slit.

"Oh, yes, Clint, yes, now . . . now . . . "

Teasing her, he put his lips to her ear and said, "You won't die, will you?"

"I don't know," she gasped. "I've never . . . no other man has ever made me . . . feel so much. . . ."

"Let's see," he said, and rammed himself into her.

Her mouth opened as if to scream, but no sound came out, even though the cords stood out on her neck. Her arms tightened around him, her eyes widened, and she bit her bottom lip.

He plunged in and out of her wildly. If this was what she had come up here for, he was going to give it to her so that she'd always remember it.

She went wild beneath him, and he felt as if he were atop an unbroken filly—and maybe he was. It took all his strength to hold her down. Her whole body was as firm and taut as her breasts. She was an incredible young woman, strong, sensitive, eager.

He pinned her wrists to the bed and continued to move in and out of her. Her hips moved with his and she continued to gasp for breath. If he hadn't known better, he might have thought she was having some kind of an attack. Her eyes were heavy-lidded and unfocused, her nostrils were flaring, her face was flushed, and she continued to bite her bottom lip.

Suddenly she stiffened beneath him, and he knew she was about to go over the edge, so he waited for her and then went with her. She lifted her hips off the bed so high that she also lifted him, using surprising strength.

She went limp under him then and began to kiss his neck and his shoulders as he lay atop her. He made a move to roll off her, and she grabbed him and held him tightly.

"Not yet, please," she said. "I want to feel you grow soft inside me."

While he lay there on her she rubbed his buttocks, ran her hands over his back, and continued to kiss and lick the flesh of his neck and shoulders. Finally he rolled off and lay beside her.

"You didn't really want me to go, did you?" she asked.

"Yes, I did."

"But you enjoyed—"

"Just because I enjoyed myself with you doesn't mean I don't think this was wrong."

"I see."

She stood up, dressed, and then faced him.

"You know I wouldn't scream."

"No," he said, staring up at her, "I knew you would."

She smiled and said, "You're right, I would have —but maybe next time I won't have to threaten."

She went out then, and he rolled over, enjoying the way the sheet still felt warm from her and smelled of her, and he drifted off to sleep.

He really did need that rest.

Especially now.

# TWENTY

When Clint left the hotel a couple of hours later, he asked the clerk to have the sheets in his room changed. He fully intended to take Delilah back to his room later that night, and he didn't want her smelling Lisa all over the sheets.

He walked to the livery, nodded at Winder as he went through the front door, and walked to the back door, where he knew he'd find Dan Dundee sitting. What he didn't expect was to find Dundee and Julia thoroughly involved in a deep kiss.

He cleared his throat and they sprang apart, guilty looks on both their faces.

"You surprised me," Dundee said.

"Didn't mean to interrupt," Clint said. "I just hope you're keeping your eyes open once in a while."

"I'm watching," Dundee said. "Things have been quiet."

"Well, that's good. Why don't you two go and get something to eat and I'll sit here a spell."

Dundee looked at Julia and she nodded vigorously. Clint doubted very much that they would go and get something to eat. They probably had something else in mind.

"I'll be back in a couple of hours," Dundee said.

"Fine," Clint said. "Enjoy."

He watched Dundee and Julia walk through the livery, then looked over to the wagons. Things were very quiet, and he decided to walk over and see how things were.

As he approached the wagons William stepped out of one of them.

"Clint!" he called out.

"How are you doing, William?"

"Fine," the boy said, running up and stopping just short of him.

"How is everybody else?"

"Nicholas is in some pain. He's never been shot before. Does it really hurt a lot?"

"Yes," Clint said, "it really hurts a lot. How's Armando?"

"He wants to get up, but Delilah won't let him."

"And your grandparents?"

"They're fine. They're anxious to get going to meet with the others."

"I'm sure they are."

"You really want to know about Delilah, don't you?" the boy asked.

"I'm concerned about all of you."

"Yes, but more about Delilah. I see the way you look at her."

"And what do you know about the way a man looks at a woman?"

"I know how you look at her, and how she looks at you. Are you going to get married?"

"William!"

Delilah had come out of the wagon in time to hear the last question.

William turned and said, "I was just asking."

"Well, you can stop asking right now. Understand?"

"Yes, Delilah."

"Armando wants some coffee."

"I will bring it to him."

Clint waited while Delilah poured a cup of coffee and William took it to Armando.

"A cup?" she asked him.

"Sure."

She poured a cup and handed it to him, and then poured one for herself.

"What have you been up to?" she asked.

He wondered if a guilty look crossed his face.

"I talked to the doctor and the sheriff, and then I took a nap."

"A nap?"

"When you get to be my age, you need a nap every once in a while."

"Is that so?" she asked. "I'll remember that in ten or twelve years."

"How are the king and queen?"

She smiled and said, "They are fine. You think that is amusing, don't you?"

"No, no, I don't," he said. "I just never expected

to meet a king and queen in this country."

"I suppose that is a little unusual for you."

"Yes, it is."

"I see you have recruited another man to keep an eye on us."

"Oh, Dundee. You noticed him, huh?"

"How could I not? He and Julia were making eyes at each other all morning, and then she went over there to sit with him."

"I just thought it might be a good idea if they met," Clint said.

"Well, I guess it was," Delilah said. "At least it got her mind off you."

"I figured all it would take was meeting a younger man."

"She seems very pleased," Delilah said. "You wouldn't have a younger friend for me, would you?"

He looked at her and said, "I'll see what I can arrange."

"No, no," she said, "never mind. I suppose I'll just have to settle for seeing you between naps."

"I'll try to make sure I'm awake for dinner tonight," he said.

"I'll keep nudging you."

"What kind of noises is Armando making?"

"He still doesn't like or trust you. He wants to get up, he wants us to leave town," she said. "I'm trying to keep him on his back as long as possible."

"Not the same way you keep me on my back, I hope," he said.

"No," Delilah said, "I just sit on him—I *straddle* you."

"Yes, I know," he said. "I rather enjoy that. Tell me something."

"What?"

"Who's in line to be king after Ivan?"

"Armando is his closest male blood relative."

"And he's already trying to act like king."

She shrugged and said, "Maybe. I think he's just trying to do what's right for us."

"Well, I hope so."

He handed her back the coffee cup and turned to leave.

"Where are you going now?"

"I'm just going to sit over here at my post and wait for Dundee to come back."

"With Julia."

"Yeah," he said, "with Julia."

As he was walking away she called out to him, "That could take hours."

# TWENTY-ONE

Jack Weeks regarded the ten men he had picked, much the way a commanding officer studies his troops.

"We got any Gypsy lovers here?" he asked.

"Their women, maybe," somebody said, and everyone else laughed.

"I don't need funny men," Weeks said, staring at the man who had spoken. "You want out, Nelson?"

"No, boss."

"Because this is going to mean a lot to Mr. Gordon," Weeks said. "He's gonna remember the men who helped him out on this."

Weeks studied the man further, and they all remained silent, waiting.

"All right," Weeks said, "now there's one other thing you should all know."

He paused, then went on.

"There's a man named Clint Adams involved. Do you fellas know who Clint Adams is?"

They all exchanged glances, and then one of them said, "Sure, boss. They call him the Gunsmith."

"That's right."

"Uh, are we gonna have to go up against him?"

"Maybe," Weeks said. "If it comes to that, everybody gets a bonus."

"Uh, if we live to collect it."

That was Nelson again, and Weeks pinned him with a hard stare.

"Uh, Nelson's right, boss," another man said.

"That's right, Kyle," Weeks said. "That's why the money involved in the bonus will be *big* money."

Weeks walked back and forth in front of the men, who he had lined up inside the barn.

"If anyone wants out, now's the time to say so— but . . . if you do pull out, you'd better pull out all the way. I don't want anybody working for Mr. Gordon who's not willing to go all the way for him."

Weeks studied them, then looked at Nelson and said, "What about you, Nelson?"

"I could use a big bonus, boss," Nelson said, "and we *are* talking about a bunch of Gypsies and one man."

"Kyle?"

"I'm in, boss."

"And the rest of you?"

There was a general nodding of heads and murmuring of assent.

"Good," Weeks said, "now here's what we're going to do . . ."

•    •    •

Lisa Gordon watched from her window as ten men filed into the barn, followed by Jack Weeks, and then an hour later as they all filed out again, followed again by Jack Weeks.

All she could think was that the preceding hour spelled bad news for Clint Adams and his friends, the Gypsies. She didn't know why her father hated Gypsies, but she knew that if Weeks and his men went after them, Clint Adams was going to get in their way—and maybe get hurt.

She had to warn him.

As he left the barn Jack Weeks looked up and thought he saw some movement in Lisa's window. He tried to keep looking without seeming to, and saw her head pop into view again and then jerk away real quick.

Weeks was aware that Lisa had been in town that afternoon. Although he didn't know exactly why she had been there, he didn't like the fact that she had gone in alone.

If Lisa Gordon was peeking out windows, Weeks thought maybe he should bring it to her father's attention.

Now that Weeks had finished his meeting with the ten men he'd chosen to run the Gypsies out of town, he went around to the back of the house, where three other men were waiting.

As he approached, two of the men put out cigarettes they'd been smoking while they waited.

"All right," Jack Weeks said, "you men know you weren't hired for your abilities to punch cows. You were hired for jobs like the one I'm going to give you now."

"Just name it, Jack," Verne Gagne said.

Verne Gagne, Rick Rice, and Bob Morton all had been hired because they knew how to handle a gun, and there were times when Sam Gordon needed men like that. Gordon had left it up to Weeks to hire the right kind of men, and Weeks had come up with these three.

"You fellas know who Clint Adams is?"

All three suddenly came to attention, and Gagne said, "We're talking about the Gunsmith."

"That's right," Weeks said. "What would you fellas think about getting a chance at the Gunsmith?"

Rice and Morton exchanged smiles, and Gagne, speaking for the three of them, said, "Just point us in his direction."

# TWENTY-TWO

Dinner was just a preamble to what they both knew was waiting for them in Clint's room.

"This night is a treasure," Delilah whispered to Clint while her mouth roamed his body, "because I never expected to have it—and now we'll have another tomorrow too."

"That means we can take our time," Clint said, reaching for her. Her mouth had been teasing him for ten minutes, and that was long enough. He lifted her up onto him, and she slid herself over him and took him inside.

She sat up straight on him, her breasts thrust out, and he thumbed her nipples while she rode him. . . .

Gagne, Rice, and Morton rode into town after dark and left their horses behind the hotel. They had already discussed what they were going to do, so there was no need for them to speak.

Rice and Morton forced the back door of the hotel and went inside, while Gagne climbed to the low roof in back of the hotel and made his way around to the side of the hotel. They knew which room was Clint Adams's, and that's where they were headed.

Clint had reversed their position and Delilah was now on the bottom, clawing at him, imploring him to drive himself even deeper into her.

Clint had very rarely indulged in mindless sex. He had that afternoon with Lisa Gordon, and it was fortunate that there was nothing else around that needed his attention.

Now, even as he was driving into Delilah, he was aware of his surroundings, which was no reflection on Delilah at all. The situation with Lisa had been unexpected, and his reaction had surprised even himself.

Clint heard the creaking of the floor out in the hall, and he heard the roof outside his window creaking.

He put his lips near Delilah's ear and said, "When I tell you, roll onto the floor."

"The floor?" she gasped. "Why—"

"Just do it!" he snapped, and she knew then that something was wrong.

Clint reached up to the bedpost and took his gun out of his holster.

"Get ready," Clint whispered to her.

He heard whoever was out in the hall stop at his door, and knew then that he was right.

The door flew open as someone kicked it, and he

shouted to Delilah, "Now!" and pushed her to his left, away from the door.

He turned on the bed and fired at the door, three shots in quick seccession.

When he heard the window break, he heard Delilah cry out. He turned and saw the muzzle flash of a gun from the window as he pulled the trigger of his own gun.

He turned to the door again quickly. There was some light coming in from the lamps in the hall, but there was no one standing in the doorway. There *was* a man lying on the floor, but that was all.

"Delilah?"

"I'm all right," she said.

"Stay on the floor."

Clint jumped off the bed and went to the window. The low roof outside slanted down, so if he hit whoever was out there, they either had fallen off or gotten away. The blood on the windowsill told him that he had in fact hit someone with his shot.

He went to the doorway next and cautiously peered out into the hall. There were other people sticking their heads out their doors, but no one was anxious to come out into the hall and get hit by flying lead.

He turned up the lamp on the wall by the door and then bent over to examine the man on the floor. He had two holes in his chest and was quite dead. He had fired three shots at the door, and a look out into the hall showed a trail of blood down the hall leading to the back stairs.

Now he turned and went back into the room to check on Delilah.

"Are you all right?" he asked, helping her up.

"I got hit by some glass," she said.

She sat on the bed, and he examined her, finding some lacerations on her left thigh. The glass had either hit her on the fly or she had rolled onto it while it lay on the floor.

"It's not bad," Clint said.

"I know," she said, putting her hand on his shoulder. "Are you all right?"

"I'm fine," he said. "One of them is dead, and it seems that there were two others, who are both wounded. We'd better get some clothes on. The sheriff should be here soon."

"All right," she said, "but afterward we can go back to what we were doing—if you're willing."

"You're incredible," he said. He kissed her and said, "Yes, I'm willing."

Outside the window, Verne Gagne had taken a bullet in the hip and managed to avoid falling off the roof. He retraced his steps, not knowing whether or not Clint Adams had taken a hit.

He only knew that he had.

Rick Rice made his way down the back steps, holding his hand to his bloody shoulder. He had never seen anybody move as fast as Clint Adams had. When he and Morton had kicked the door open, he had felt sure they had the drop on Adams, and then bang, Morton was on the floor and had a bullet in his shoulder.

Maybe Gagne had managed to get Adams from the window.

• • •

When Gagne and Rice met behind the hotel, they looked at each other and knew that Adams had taken the three of them. They climbed up onto their horses and headed away from Virginia City—and away from Jack Weeks.

Weeks could get somebody else to go after the Gunsmith.

# TWENTY-THREE

"Looks like you and the lady got pretty lucky," Sheriff Randle said.

"Luck had nothing to do with it," Delilah said.

Randle looked at Clint.

"You mean to say, you knew they were coming after you?" the lawman asked.

"Let's just say I'm not surprised."

"Well, I had the dead fella hauled off to the undertaker's."

"I'd like to go over and take a look at him in the morning," Clint said.

"He's not going anywhere."

"Did you know him, Sheriff?"

"No, never saw him before."

"You mean, he doesn't work for Sam Gordon?"

"Not that I know of."

"Are you sure?"

"Dammit, Adams," the sheriff said, and then seemed to realize who he was talking to. "I mean— look, if I knew that man was one of Gordon's, I'd tell you."

"That depends."

"Depends on what?"

"Depends on who you're more afraid of, him or me."

Randle didn't know what to say to that, and looked for something in the room to look at. Delilah was sitting on the bed, fully dressed except for her bare feet, so he stared at her feet. Even *they* were beautiful, like the rest of her.

"All right, Sheriff," Clint said.

"Huh?" Randle said, yanking his eyes away from Delilah's feet.

"I think you're finished here now."

"Oh, sure," Randle said. "I'll tell the undertaker you'll be by in the morning."

"Thanks."

"Oh, what about the window? You want me to tell the manager to put you in another room?"

"No," Clint said, "the night air will do us good."

Randle took one more quick look at Delilah's feet and then left.

Clint turned around and said to Delilah, "He liked your feet."

"I noticed."

He sat on the bed with her and began to unbutton her shirt. He was wearing only his jeans.

"What about the window, Clint?" she asked. "What if those men come back?"

"They won't," he said, kissing her cheek.

"They're off licking their wounds." He kissed her other cheek, then both her eyes, her nose, and her mouth. She opened her mouth wide beneath his and let her tongue flick out into his mouth.

When he had her undressed, he paused to remove his jeans and then lay down beside her.

"You don't like scaring people, do you?" she said.

"Who did I scare?"

"You scared the sheriff."

"He scares himself," Clint said. "People who are frightened are usually more frightened by themselves than by other people."

"Aren't you ever frightened?"

"Sure," Clint said. "There have been times when I've been scared out of my wits, but there was always something to be frightened of; I didn't conjure something up. People like the sheriff are afraid before they *know* that there's something to be afraid of."

"Gypsies are like that."

"Like what?"

"Afraid before they know there's something to be afraid of. We were afraid when you rode up on us, and we knew nothing about you."

"That might be different."

"How?"

"You probably have cause to fear strangers."

"Yes, we do," she said, "but we shouldn't live like that."

"You shouldn't have to," Clint said, "but maybe you have no choice."

She looked at him then and said, "You understand, don't you?"

She kissed him before he could answer, a long,

lingering thank-you kiss that quickly deepened into something else.

Jack Weeks waited until almost midnight, and then he knew that the three men were not coming back. They were either dead or running. He'd find out which when he went into town the next day.

He had kept Gagne, Rice, and Morton away from town, so no one would be able to connect any of them with him or the S&G.

Now it was going to be up to him and the ten men he'd picked.

Maybe they could defeat Adams by sheer weight of numbers.

# TWENTY-FOUR

Clint went to the undertaker's in the morning, after walking Delilah back to the Gypsies' wagons. The undertaker, a wizened old man named Paul Fixx, pulled back the sheet and showed Clint the body of the man he'd killed the night before.

"Know 'im?" Fixx asked.

"No. You?"

"Never seen him before."

Clint looked dispassionately at the two neat holes in the man's chest.

"Heard he took you by surprise in your hotel room," Fixx said.

"That was his intent."

Fixx held his hand over the two wounds and covered them both.

"That's pretty good shooting."

Clint didn't comment.

"Guess he must have known you, huh?"

"I don't think so," Clint said. "Cover him up."

"Sure, sure," Fixx said, and pulled the sheet back over him.

"If anyone comes looking for him, I want to know about it."

"Well, I'll have to tell the sheriff . . ."

Clint looked at the undertaker and said, "You tell me first, understand? Even before the sheriff."

"Uh, sure, mister, you first."

"My name's Adams. I'm at the hotel."

"Sure, mister, sure."

Clint left the undertaker's and saw Sheriff Randle walking toward him.

"Morning, Sheriff."

"Mr. Adams," the sheriff said, "I was just comin' over here to see if maybe you recognized that feller today."

"No, I didn't, Sheriff," Clint said. "He's nobody from my past, if that's what you were hoping. To my way of thinking, he was hired to do what he did, he and his two friends."

"And you figure by Mr. Gordon?"

"Or somebody working for him."

"Why?"

"To get me out of the way so they could run off the Gypsies."

"You think Mr. Gordon hates those Gypsies enough to kill you?"

"That's what I think, Sheriff."

"Well . . ."

"And if I find some way to prove it, I expect you to act."

"How do you mean . . . act?" Randle asked cautiously.

"I mean that if I can prove that Gordon hired those men, I expect you to arrest him for conspiracy to commit murder."

"Is that a crime? I never heard of that."

"It's a crime."

"Pretty fancy-sounding."

"Murder's murder, no matter how you fancy it up."

"And you expect Mr. Gordon to be tried here, and convicted?"

"No, I imagine I'd try to find some way to have him tried elsewhere, where he doesn't own the judge, jury . . . *and* the law."

"Hey—"

"Just remember, Sheriff," Clint said. "When I find that proof, I'll be bringing it to you. Now excuse me."

Clint walked away from the lawman without giving him a chance to say anything else.

He went to the livery to see if Dan Dundee was there yet and found the young man at his post.

"Heard there was some excitement last night," Dundee said.

"Yeah," Clint said, "I had a visitor or two."

"Got one of them?"

"Yeah."

"Know him?"

"No, but I'm pretty sure he had to be working for Gordon."

"Anybody recognize him as one of Gordon's men?"

"No."

"I could take a look at him," Dundee said. "I worked out there for three weeks."

"That's right," Clint said, wondering why he hadn't thought of that himself. "Dan, go over and take a look at the body and see if you *do* recognize him. If I can tie him to Gordon, maybe I can hurt Gordon with it."

"I'll get over there right now," Dundee said, getting up from the chair that Old Man Winder must have supplied him.

"I'll take over here."

Clint took up a position by the back door from which he could see the wagons.

His hope was that Dundee would recognize the man right away and he'd be able to put enough pressure on Sam Gordon that he would forget all about harassing the Gypsies.

# TWENTY-FIVE

Jack Weeks rode into town and spotted Dan Dundee crossing the street.

"Dundee!"

Dundee looked up at the sound of his name and saw Weeks riding toward him.

"What do you want, Weeks?"

Weeks stopped his horse and dismounted.

"Take it easy, Dundee," Weeks said. "I just want to talk to you."

"What about?"

"We haven't had a chance to talk since that fiasco the other day," Weeks said. "How come you never came back to the ranch?"

"I assumed I was fired."

"What made you assume that?"

"What else would happen after I went against your men?" Dundee asked.

"Yeah, but my men were wrong," Weeks said, "and you were right."

"Is that a fact?"

"Yeah, it is. They were told never to hurt anyone or attack any women—"

"They did it on their own, huh?"

"That's right," Weeks said, "and you know why? They didn't have a leader."

"That's too bad."

"You could have been that leader, Dundee."

"I only worked for you for three weeks, Jack," Dundee said. "What makes you think they would have listened to what I had to say?"

"We can arrange it so they listen to you, Dan," Weeks said.

"That would mean my coming back."

"Of course."

"Which I'm not about to do."

"And why not?"

"Because I worked out there for three weeks, and that was long enough. I don't like the way things are done at the S&G, Weeks. I don't like you, and I don't like Sam Gordon."

Weeks turned red in the face and glared at Dundee.

"I heard you're squiring one of those Gypsy gals around town."

"That's none of your business."

"And having drinks with Clint Adams?"

"Who I drink with is my business, Weeks."

"I'm just warning you, Dundee," Weeks said. "You're mixing in with the wrong element."

"No, Weeks," Dundee said, "I *was* mixing in with the wrong element, but now I'm on the right side."

"The right side is the strong side, Dundee," Weeks said, "and you ain't exactly on the strong side."

"Why don't you take a walk, Weeks. I think we've finished our conversation."

"We've finished it, all right," Weeks said. "Remember that I tried to be a nice guy and gave you warning, Dundee."

"Sure, Weeks," Dundee said, "you're a helluva nice guy. Everybody knows that."

Dundee walked away from Jack Weeks, and Weeks watched him, wondering how differently he should have approached him. If he could have turned Dundee, he could have made good use of the fact that Adams and the Gypsies trusted him.

Weeks watched Dundee cross the street, and when he realized where he was going, he suddenly wondered how well Gagne, Rice, and Morton had managed to stay away from the other men on the S&G spread.

If Dundee recognized the dead Morton, things might get very complicated.

"This fella sure is popular today," Paul Fixx said.

"Just take the sheet off him."

"I wonder if he was this popular when he was alive?" Fixx said.

Dundee studied the body on the table very closely, trying very hard to put a name to the face, because the face was very familiar.

He knew that all he had to do was tell Clint that the dead man worked for Gordon, and Clint would be able to go to the sheriff with that, but at the moment he just wasn't sure. The face *was* familiar, but was it familiar from his three weeks as an employee of Sam Gordon or for some other reason?

"Cover him up," Dundee said.

"Do you know him?"

"No," Dundee said. "No, I don't know him—not yet."

Fixx laughed and said, "Well, if you don't know him now, you sure ain't got any time to *get* to know him."

Frowning, Dundee left the undertaker's and headed back to the livery.

That damn face was so familiar!

Weeks saw Dundee leave the undertaker's office, and he saw the frown on the man's face.

"Dammit, he thought, Dundee *knows* him, but he can't figure out from where yet.

Weeks's men hadn't been successful in removing Clint Adams from the land of the living, and right now Dundee was even more dangerous than Adams was.

Weeks had three men coming into town just a half hour behind him. He was going to have to promise them a *big* bonus.

# TWENTY-SIX

Clint was disappointed, but he understood Dan Dundee's predicament. The younger man did not want to *say* he recognized the dead man from Sam Gordon's ranch if he wasn't sure.

"I'm sorry, Clint."

"Don't worry about it, Dan," Clint said. "If it does come to you, let me know."

"Sure," Dan said, "I just wish—"

"Forget it, Dan. You can't swear to something if you don't know it for sure."

Clint left the livery and went to the hotel dining room to have breakfast. When he walked in, he saw Jack Weeks sitting at a table and went over.

"Chow out at the ranch that bad?" he asked.

"Adams," Weeks said. "Take a seat."

"You're inviting me to eat with you?"

"Sure, why not?" Weeks said. "I've got nothing against you personally."

Clint sat down opposite the S&G foreman, who was having a breakfast of bacon and eggs. A waiter came over and Clint said, "I'll have the same thing he's having."

"Yes, sir."

After the waiter left, Weeks said, "You know, we don't have any beef against each other."

"We don't, huh?"

"Naw," Weeks said, "it's Gordon and those Gypsies that have a beef. You and me, we're just stuck in the middle."

"Why don't we get out of the middle?"

"Yeah, yeah," Weeks said, "that's what I was going to say. You know, it can be real profitable, getting out of the middle."

"Are you asking me to pay you to get out of the middle?"

"Naw," Weeks said, waving his hand, "I know you can't pay me what Gordon's paying me, but he can sure pay you a bundle to step aside."

"There's only one problem with that," Clint said.

"What's that?"

"If I took the money, I wouldn't be able to carry it around with me."

"Why not?" Weeks asked, frowning.

"Because of the stink."

Weeks sat up straight and stared hard at Clint.

"Oh, no offense, right?" Clint said, "After all, it's Sam Gordon's money we're talking about, right?"

"Yeah," Weeks said. "Gordon's money, and a lot of it."

"Just to step aside and let him run the Gypsies out of town, right?"

"That's right."

The waiter came with Clint's breakfast then, and they suspended conversation until he had laid everything out and left.

"Tell me something, Weeks."

"What?"

"Why doesn't Gordon just offer that money to the Gypsies to leave?"

"Gordon pay Gypsies?" Weeks said. "Man, that would never happen."

"What has he got against Gypsies?"

"Well," Weeks said, "I'll tell you, but if you ever tell *him* I told you, I'll deny it."

"He and I don't talk much," Clint said, stuffing some eggs and bacon into his mouth.

"When he was younger," Weeks said, "he had himself a pretty wife. Not Lisa's mother but his first wife, and they had themselves a little ranch."

"Yeah, so?"

"Well, a bunch of Gypsies camped near their house, and Gordon and his wife . . . well, they were real nice to these Gypsies. Gave them food and water, were real hospitable."

"So?"

"So? When those Gypsies pulled up stakes and left, Gordon's pretty little wife left with them. Seems one of them Gypsies was a real handsome fella with curly, dark hair and an earring, and he and Gordon's wife really took to each other."

Clint stared at Weeks.

"What?" Weeks said.

"Is that story true?"

"Oh, it's true," Weeks said. "The old man got drunk one night and told me. Why?"

"Well, now at least I understand why he had such a hatred of Gypsies."

"Does that mean you're willing to step aside now?"

"No, it doesn't."

"I don't understand you, Adams," Weeks said. "What are these people to you?"

"Friends."

"Friends? You just met them a couple of days ago."

"I make friends real fast."

"I guess you do."

They didn't seem to have much to talk about after that, and each finished eating his breakfast as if the other one wasn't there. When Weeks called for the check, Clint insisted on paying for his own meal.

"Why? I invited you to sit down."

"If you paid for my breakfast, Weeks," Clint said, standing up and taking out his money, "you'd be paying with Gordon's money."

"It's my money."

"You get paid by Gordon," Clint said. "Let's just say the food would stay down better if I paid for it myself." He handed the waiter the money and then said to Weeks, "No offense."

"Sure," Weeks said, "no offense, Adams."

On the way out Clint passed three men in the lobby who looked him over. He saw them but ignored them. He'd remember their faces, though— just in case.

The three men entered the dining room and saw Jack Weeks sitting at a table drinking coffee.

"Hi, boss," one of them said.

"Sit down, Nelson," Weeks said. All three men pulled up chairs and sat down.

"Was that him leaving?" Nelson asked. "The Gunsmith?"

"That was him."

"He don't look so tough," one of/the other men said.

"Don't let his looks fool you, Kyle," Weeks said. "Look, I've got something for you to do before you take care of Clint Adams."

"What's that?"

"It involves an old friend of yours," Weeks said. "Dan Dundee."

"That turncoat!" Nelson said, and the other two agreed.

"I thought that might interest you," Weeks said. "Here's what I want done with him—exactly the way I say. . . ."

# TWENTY-SEVEN

"That wheel should be here this afternoon," Winder told Clint.

"It made good time."

"Your Gypsy friends should be ready to go by morning."

"They'll be glad to hear that," Clint said. "Where's Dundee?"

"He's back there, last I saw."

Clint walked to the back and found Dundee sitting in his chair.

"Quiet?" he asked.

"Very," Dundee said. "I haven't had any luck digging up a name, or a place, to go with the face."

"That's okay."

"What have you been up to?"

"Breakfast," Clint said, "with Jack Weeks."

"Weeks?" Dundee said. "Why'd you eat with him?"

Clint told him about Weeks offering him money to step aside.

"Looks like he tried to buy us both off," Dundee said, and told Clint about *his* conversation with Weeks.

"Well, now that he couldn't buy us, he's going to try to push us."

"Did Winder tell you about the wheel?"

"He did."

"Why not just tell Gordon about it," Dundee said. "He ought to be real happy that they'll be leaving tomorrow."

"I don't know."

"Why?"

"I think he wants to push them and keep pushing. I don't think he wants them to leave on their own; he wants to *run* them out."

"Fine," Dundee said. "Let him think he's running them out tomorrow."

"We'll see if that satisfies him."

"I hope it does," Dundee said, "although I'll be sorry to see them go."

"Me too."

"Will you be leaving too?"

"Yes."

"Going their way?"

Clint thought about that for a moment, then said, "I don't think so."

"Why not?"

"I wouldn't want them to get too used to having me around."

"Don't want to get too involved, huh?"

"That's it."

"Maybe I'll travel with them a ways," Dundee said. "I wouldn't mind getting a little involved."

"With Julia?"

"Uh-huh."

"She's a beautiful girl."

"She sure is."

"You'll have to win Armando over, though."

"Which one's that?"

"The one with the headache," Clint said. "He's in line to be king after old Ivan."

"Is he hard to win over?"

"Not if you're a Gypsy."

"Well, he's been up and around today."

"Doing what?"

"Just walking. Came in to talk to Winder about the wheel and he told him he'd be ready to leave tomorrow. I guess that means you'll have your wheel back, huh?"

"I guess so."

"I'll stay here most of the day if you want," Dundee said. "Julia will be by later."

"It's just as well," Clint said. "Weeks is in town with some of his men. Maybe I ought to keep an eye on him."

"Maybe the last day will be uneventful."

"Now there's a case of wishful thinking if I ever heard one."

Clint left the livery, wondering if there was any chance of Dundee's wish coming true, but if there was, then what was Weeks doing in town with some of his boys?

Clint was walking down the street when he saw Lisa Gordon go into his hotel.

"Oh, no," he said to himself, "not again. Not this time."

He hurried to the hotel and caught her before she left the lobby.

"Lisa!" he said.

She turned and ran to him when she saw him, grabbing his arm.

"Quick, we have to go to your room."

"We can't, Lisa, not again—"

"Not for that, you fool!" she said, looking around. "Jack Weeks might be in town."

"He is. In fact, he was having breakfast here in the dining room."

"Come on," she said, tightening her grip on his arm. "We have to go to your room, where we won't be seen together."

"All right."

They went up the stairs to his room and inside. When he had the door closed behind them, he said, "All right, we're here, but if you touch me, *I'll* scream."

"You have to get away, Clint," she said.

"Why?"

"Because Weeks has gathered about ten of his men together for some reason, and I'm sure it has to do with those Gypsies. If they go after them, I know you'll get in the middle."

"You're right."

"And you'll get killed."

"Maybe not."

"What can you do against ten men?"

"I don't know, but what can the Gypsies do against them?" Clint studied the girl for a moment and wondered how much she knew. "Lisa, do you know why your father hates Gypsies?"

"No . . . do you?"

"No." He decided he wouldn't be the one to tell her the story.

"All right, Lisa," Clint said, "now that you've warned me, get back to your father's ranch."

"Don't I get a reward?" she asked.

"I don't have time—"

"I'll settle for a kiss."

"All right."

He leaned over to kiss her lightly, but she grabbed him by the neck and mashed her ripe mouth against his. She pushed her tongue past his lips and proceeded to take his breath away.

"Lisa . . ." he said, pushing her away.

"I'm going," she said. "Stay alive, please?"

"That is always my intention."

# TWENTY-EIGHT

Clint let Lisa leave ahead of him so that they wouldn't be seen together, but that wasn't much help. When she got down to the lobby, Jack Weeks was coming out of the dining room.

"Lisa?" he said.

She turned quickly and stared at Jack Weeks. She was determined not to be intimidated or put on the defensive by him.

"What are you doing here?" he asked.

"I could ask you the same thing."

"Don't do that, Lisa," he said. "I asked you a question."

"And I don't have to answer it."

He grabbed her by the arm as she turned away and said, "Oh, yes, you do!"

"Jack, let me go."

"What are you doing here?"

"I was visiting a friend," she said, still trying to pull away from him.

"Clint Adams? Is that your friend?"

"None of your business. Let me go!"

"Lisa, what will your father say—"

"I'm sure you'll tell him and find out," she said. "Jack, let me go," she screamed, and slapped him in the face.

He got this real shocked look on his face, and then his eyes widened and she knew he was going to hit her.

He spun her around and raised his right hand to strike her, but over his shoulder she saw Clint Adams come up behind him.

Clint grabbed Weeks, spun him around, and hit him in the jaw. Lisa had to scamper out of the way to avoid being hit by Weeks as he staggered back from the blow.

He righted himself and his hand streaked for his gun before he realized what he was doing.

"Don't do it, Weeks!" Clint snapped.

Weeks's hand stopped as it came into contact with the butt of his gun and he suddenly realized who he was facing. He took his hand away from his gun and wiped his mouth with it, smearing the back of his hand with blood.

"I'll remember this, Adams," Weeks said, "and Mr. Gordon will hear about it."

As Weeks went out the front door, Clint called out, "Does this mean that we *do* have a personal beef now?"

Weeks was out the door, though, and either didn't hear the remark or ignored it.

"Clint, he's going to kill you—"

"He might try," Clint said, "but you won't be here to see it. You'd better get on home."

"But Jack—"

"He'll be in town a while longer, Lisa," Clint said. "You have to get to your father before he does and make sure he knows the truth."

"And what will you do?"

"Just what you said."

"What?"

"Stay alive."

Weeks was of two minds.

On one hand, after what had just happened in the hotel lobby, he wanted to kill Clint Adams himself. Hell, Lisa had been in his room! Who knew what they were doing in there?

On the other hand, he had already put a plan into effect, and moving against Clint Adams now might ruin it.

He would have to wait until he was finished with the Gypsies before he moved against Clint.

As for Lisa, he was going to have to tell her father what had happened and convince him that she needed a husband to look after her and that *he* should be that husband. By marrying Lisa he would be getting the woman he wanted and assure himself of one day getting the whole ranch for himself.

But before all of that he had to make sure of one thing.

That Clint Adams was dead.

# TWENTY-NINE

When the wheel arrived, Ivan and Maria had to leave their wagon while the new wheel was put on. Clint offered to take them to a restaurant for lunch, and Delilah managed to convince them to go. William accompanied them, and Julia chose to stay with Dan Dundee, who would continue to watch the wagon that Armando and Nicholas were in.

Jack Weeks's man, Nelson, watched while Clint Adams and some of the Gypsies walked away from the wagons, leaving one empty. He could also see Dan Dundee at the back door of the livery with the youngest Gypsy girl. That meant that one of the wagons was empty.

Nelson sneaked up on the wagon from the blind side and entered. He began looking around and finally found what he wanted: a knife with a real fancy

145

handle. It had red and blue jewels in it, and if he had been just a thief, it would have been a find.

Instead it was a find for a totally different reason.

William convinced Ivan and Maria to have steak, so they *all* had steak. Once the Gypsies got back on the road, young William was going to miss his lunches with Clint.

When they returned to the livery area, Clint could see Winder and the big man who worked for him finishing up with the new wheel. Armando and Nicholas had come out of their wagon to watch. If the Gypsies wanted to, they could leave town today and go as far as they could until dark.

They were all approaching the wagons when they heard the scream.

Clint looked around, but when Delilah said, "That's Julia!" he knew where to look.

He broke from the crowd and ran to the back door of the livery. Julia was standing there with both hands clenched into fists and pressed to her mouth. Her eyes were wide with terror. Lying at her feet was Dan Dundee.

Sticking out of Dundee's back was a knife with a jewel-encrusted handle.

Delilah came up behind Clint and took Julia into her arms. When her eyes fell on Dundee, she gasped.

Clint turned and looked at her and asked, "Do you know whose knife that is?"

"Yes," she said, staring at him with puzzled eyes. "It's King Ivan's."

# THIRTY

They were all in the sheriff's office, and for a change Randle was acting like a sheriff.

"Now look," Randle said, "Dundee was seen around town with this young girl—"

"Julia," Delilah said. "Her name is Julia."

Delilah had her arms around Julia, who was still sobbing.

"Yeah, Julia," Randle said, "and she was seen going into his hotel with him."

"So?" Clint said. "Is that supposed to give her a motive to kill him? She's got a lump on the back of her head, Sheriff. That supports her story that she was hit before Dundee was killed."

"I ain't saying she killed him," Randle said, "but he *was* killed by a Gypsy knife, so one of these people had to have killed him."

"Well, four of them were with me at lunch," Clint said.

"Which four?"

Clint told the sheriff about Ivan and Maria and Delilah and William going to lunch with him.

"That leaves this fella," Randle said, "and his brother."

"His brother has been on his back for two days with a bullet wound in his shoulder," Clint said.

"Well, then, that leaves him," Randle said, pointing to Armando, "and I got to arrest somebody or this town's gonna explode."

"I killed no one," Armando said.

"Why would he kill Dundee?"

"Maybe he didn't want Dundee seeing this little gal here."

"You can't arrest him, Sheriff," Clint said.

"Why not?"

"Because you have no evidence."

"I have the knife."

"Which doesn't belong to him."

"But he had—whaddayacallit?—access to it."

"So did a lot of people," Clint said. "That wagon was empty while the new wheel was being put on— and come to think of it, he and his brother were watching the wheel being put on."

"I will think on it," Randle said.

"Meanwhile," Clint said, standing up, "we're leaving."

"You can leave my office, Mr. Adams," Randle said, "but these Gypsies can't leave town. I might have to call in some help on this, maybe a federal marshal. I can't let them leave town."

"All right, Sheriff," Clint said. "You call in someone who knows what he's doing. Meanwhile I'll do some nosing around of my own."

Clint walked to the door, opened it, and allowed all of the Gypsies to precede him out the door.

"Adams, don't let them kill anyone else."

"You're trying to act like a real a sheriff now, Randle," Clint said. "My guess is it's for Gordon's benefit. Just don't push it too far, huh? Remember, you're the sheriff, not a detective—and you're not much of a sheriff."

Armando and Delilah were waiting for Clint outside.

"Ivan and Maria took Julia and William back to the wagons," Delilah said.

"We must leave town at once," Armando said.

"If you leave town now, Armando," Clint said, "there'll be a posse after you before sundown."

"What do we do?" Delilah asked.

"You don't do anything," Clint said, "any of you. You go back to the wagons and wait for me."

"We cannot wait for him," Armando said. "The people of this town will believe that we killed that man. We are not safe here."

Both Clint and Delilah ignored Armando.

"What are you going to do?" Delilah asked.

"I'm going to find out who really killed Dan Dundee," Clint said, "and when I do, he's going to be a very sorry man."

"You think it was Gordon?" Delilah asked.

"No," Clint said. "I don't think Gordon had any reason to want Dundee dead."

"Why not? He hates us."

"But he wants you out of Virginia City," Clint said. "By framing you for murder, all he does is keep you in town. No, it wasn't Gordon, but it might have been somebody working for him. If it was, he's going to be on our side in this."

"You're going to see him?"

"Yes."

"All right," Delilah said, "we'll go back to the wagons."

"We should leave town—" Armando said.

"See if you can get him to stop thinking like that," Clint said.

"Adams—"

"Come, Armando," Delilah said, "Clint is trying to help us."

"We do not need his help."

"Don't be an idiot . . ." she said to him, but Clint was already walking away and didn't hear the rest of it.

# THIRTY-ONE

Clint rode out to the Gordon ranch, wondering if Jack Weeks and Lisa Gordon had returned from town yet.

He was apprehensive about leaving the Gypsies unprotected, but Randle was going to have to do his best to keep the townspeople off them, or the town *would* explode. He also didn't feel that the real killer would go after them so soon.

As he approached the house, no one stepped out to meet him. He tied Duke to a post in front of the house and went to the front door. He knocked and was surprised when the door was opened by Gordon himself.

"What do you want?"

"I want to talk to you."

"About what?"

"About murder."

"What?" Gordon asked, suddenly looking concerned. "Lisa's not here. You don't mean—"

"No, not Lisa, although she was in town—"

"What did you do to her?"

"I kept Jack Weeks from backhanding her."

"Weeks? What are you talking about?" Gordon demanded. "Who was murdered?"

"A man who used to work for you," Clint said. "Dan Dundee."

"That traitor? Who killed him?"

"I don't know," Clint said, "but someone made it look like one of the Gypsies did it."

"I wouldn't be surprised."

"Well, they didn't do it. They had no reason. You, on the other hand, did."

"Me? Why would I want to kill Dundee?"

"He went against you, didn't he?"

"I don't kill men who turn against me, Adams, I fire them."

"Well, to tell you the truth, Gordon," Clint Adams said, "I don't think you really had anything to do with Dundee's death."

Gordon narrowed his eyes and studied Clint for a long moment.

"Come inside, Adams," he finally said. "There's no point in talking out here."

Clint followed Gordon to his office.

"Tell me why you came here," Gordon said. "It wasn't just to tell me that Dundee's dead."

"No," Clint said, "I came to find out who killed him."

"Well, tell me why you don't think I had anything to do with it."

"You want the Gypsies out of Virginia City," Clint

said. "Framing them for murder just keeps them here that much longer."

"You've got that right," Gordon said. "Who do you think killed Dundee?"

"I think Jack Weeks had something to do with it."

"Why Weeks?"

"Three men tried to kill me last night," Clint said, "and I managed to kill one of them."

"I didn't hear anything about that," Gordon said.

"Well, I think the man I killed worked for you."

"Was he identified as an employee of mine?"

"Not exactly."

"What does that mean?"

"Dan Dundee took a look at him and recognized him, but he couldn't put his finger on where he had seen him, or his name. I think he saw him out here while he was working here."

"What has that got to do with Dundee being killed?"

"I don't think Weeks *wanted* Dundee to remember," Clint said. "I think he had Dundee killed and had it done so that the Gypsies would get the blame."

Gordon thought about that for a few moments, rubbing a hand over his face, and then said, "If Weeks did that, then he's fired."

"How will you know?"

"I'll come to town and look at the dead man," Gordon said. "If he was on my payroll, I'll know it."

"Fair enough."

"That won't prove that Weeks had Dundee killed, though."

"No," Clint said, "but I'll work on that myself."

Gordon rose and said, "If you wait, I'll ride back to town with you."

"I want you to know one thing."

"What's that?"

"If you identify the man as having worked for you, you might be implicating yourself in sending him and his friends to kill me."

"I'll deal with that when the time comes," Gordon said. "Come outside and wait while I have my horse saddled."

As they rode into town, Gordon asked, "What was that you said about Weeks and my daughter?"

"I was in time to keep Weeks from hitting your daughter in the hotel lobby."

"Why? Weeks wasn't to marry my daughter. Why would he hit her? And what was she doing there?"

"Your daughter is a smart girl, Gordon," Clint said. "She came to town to warn me that Weeks was planning something, and he caught her leaving the hotel."

"If this is all true," Gordon said, "I'm going to be looking for a new foreman, Adams. I might be offering you that job."

"Well, if and when you do, Gordon, I'll give you my answer. We have a few things to sort out before then."

When Clint Adams and Sam Gordon rode into town together, it created quite a stir. It was no secret that they were at odds over the Gypsies.

When Sheriff Randle saw them, his jaw fell. If Adams and Gordon had joined forces, he had even more to be afraid of than before.

What if Adams was after his job?

Jack Weeks couldn't believe his eyes when he saw

them riding right down Main Street together. Somehow Adams had gotten to Gordon first and said *something* that got the old man to ride into town with him.

Weeks was going to have to find out what Adams told Gordon about him and Lisa, or about him and the Gypsies. He wondered if Adams had convinced Gordon that he had something to do with Dan Dundee's death. If Gordon thought that was true, he might actually fire Weeks.

After all these years he might actually *fire* him— especially if Adams had told him about what happened with Lisa.

When Lisa saw Clint and her father ride into town, she couldn't believe it. The only way her father would accept Adams was if Clint had decided to step aside and let the Gypsies fend for themselves— and she never thought he would do that.

Delilah was leaning over the fire making coffee when she saw Clint and Sam Gordon ride up to the livery together. Armando came out of the wagon behind her and also saw them together.

"That is the man you want us to trust?" he asked her. "He has joined forces with our enemy."

"You don't know that," Delilah said. "Clint *said* he was going to talk to Gordon."

"And now they have come riding into town together like old friends," Armando said. "Delilah, we must leave this place. You must decide if you are Gypsy or *gajo*."

"Do not doubt my loyalties, Armando," Delilah said. "Before I decide anything, I will talk to Clint first."

• • •

Clint and Gordon walked to the undertaker's from the livery, aware of all the eyes that were on them.

"I feel like I'm on display," Sam Gordon said.

"Think of it this way: While they're all looking at us, they can't be causing trouble."

When they walked into the undertaker's, Paul Fixx said, "Well, I'll be—"

"Be quiet, old man," Gordon said. "I want to see the body of the man Adams killed."

"Can't."

"What do you mean, can't?" Gordon asked.

"Buried him."

"You what?" Clint asked.

"He was buried this morning in a plain box. Couldn't keep him around here forever."

Gordon and Clint exchanged helpless looks, and then Gordon said, "Come on, Adams, I'll buy you a drink."

# THIRTY-TWO

"We could have him dug up," Clint Adams said.

"We'd need a judge for that," Sam Gordon said.

They were sitting in the saloon at a table over two beers.

"Well, don't you own a judge hereabouts?" Clint asked.

"Contrary to what you think, Adams, I don't own Virginia City."

"Well, the sheriff sure thinks you do."

"Sheriff," Sam Gordon said. "Do you know how he ended up with that job?"

"No."

"The real sheriff was killed and Randle was his chief deputy. Come next election, he'll be out on his ear, no matter who he runs against."

"Well, then," Clint said, "I guess I can't prove anything to you today, Mr. Gordon."

"Maybe you can."

"What?"

"I'll have to talk to Lisa about Weeks, and then I'll confront Weeks. If he had a man kill Dan Dundee, I'll get it out of him."

"And what then?"

"What do you mean?"

"Will you turn him over to the sheriff?"

"Why wouldn't I?"

"Because if you do, you'll be clearing the Gypsies."

"And once they're cleared, they can be on their way," Gordon said, "and *that's* what I want."

"You've got a lot of hate in you, Gordon."

"Yeah, well," Gordon said, "did it ever occur to you that I might have good reason?"

"Yes," Clint said, "it did occur to me."

"Well, I do. You'll have to trust me in that."

Gordon finished his beer and stood up.

"I'll go find my daughter, Adams. You go look after your Gypsies."

Then Clint finished his beer and stood up.

"I guess I'll have some explaining to do," Clint said.

"About what?"

"About riding in with you," Clint said. "I'm sure they've heard about it by now."

"You really care what they think of you, don't you?"

"I don't like anybody to think I've changed sides when I haven't, Gordon."

"Neither one of us has changed sides, Adams," Gordon said. "Maybe we just got some sense."

"Maybe."

"I'll talk to you after I talk to Lisa."

"All right."

They left the saloon together and went their separate ways.

Jack Weeks, standing across the street in a doorway, saw Clint and Gordon leave the saloon. Clint walked toward the livery while Gordon seemed to be heading for the hotel. Weeks stepped down and followed Gordon.

After Lisa saw her father ride in with Clint, she decided to stay in the hotel lobby, where either one of them could find her. She had a lot to tell her father, especially about Jack Weeks.

Gordon was two blocks from the hotel, approaching an alley, when Weeks came up behind him.

"Mr. Gordon?"

Gordon turned and scowled at Weeks.

"Weeks, I been hearing a lot of things about you I don't like."

"From Clint Adams?" Weeks asked scoffingly. "The man's a liar for sure."

"Did you put your hands on my daughter?"

"Now Mr. Gordon—"

"I'm on my way to talk to her, Weeks, so don't lie to me."

"Mr. Gordon, you know how I feel about Lisa—"

"Answer the question, Weeks."

"Look, Mr. Gordon—"

"Did you have Dan Dundee killed?"

"He's fillin' your head with lies for sure—"

"And did you send three men to kill Adams?"

"Now, Mr. Gordon, you told me—"

"I never told you to kill anyone, Weeks," Gordon

said. "Never! I'll talk to you after I see Lisa."

"Mr. Gordon, can we step in here and talk some?" Weeks said, indicating the alley.

"I don't do business in alleys, Weeks. We'll talk back at the ranch."

Weeks looked around, saw that no one was looking their way, and pulled his gun.

"Into the alley, Mr. Gordon," Weeks said. "You're gonna hear me out."

"You're being very foolish, Jack," Gordon said.

"Jack, is it?" Weeks said. "Now we're on a first-name basis, *Sam*, after ten years?"

"Jack—"

"Into the alley, *Sam*."

Gordon looked down at the gun that was pointed at his belly, then up to the eyes of the man holding it, and moved into the alley.

Lisa was just going to the door of the hotel to look for Clint or her father when she heard the shot.

She knew one of them was in trouble.

Clint had almost reached the livery when *he* heard the shot, and he turned and ran back the way he came.

At the sound of the shot Sheriff Randle said, "Oh, shit!" and ran from his office.

Clint ran back to the saloon and on past, toward the hotel. He saw Lisa running toward him from the hotel.

"Lisa, where's your father?"

"I thought he was with you."

"He was on his way to the hotel to find you."

"He never got there, Clint."

Clint looked around and spotted the alley across the street.

"What's going on?" Sheriff Randle called as he came abreast of Clint.

"Let's find out, Sheriff."

Clint crossed the street and entered the alley with Lisa and Sheriff Randle behind him. The alley went all the way through to the back of the buildings on either side, but they didn't have to go that far. There was a body lying right in the center of it, and when Clint turned him over, Lisa Gordon stifled a cry with her hands.

It was Sam Gordon.

"He's been shot," Clint said, looking at the sheriff, and Lisa began to cry into her clenched fists.

"You going to try to blame this one on the Gypsies, too, Sheriff?" Clint asked.

# THIRTY-THREE

Clint was back in the sheriff's office with Randle and Lisa.

"There sure are a lot of people dying since you and those Gypsies hit town, Adams," Randle said.

"I'll take credit for the one who tried to kill me, Sheriff," Clint said.

"And who do you think killed Mr. Gordon?"

"Who else?" Clint said. "Jack Weeks."

"Why?"

"Because Gordon was about to find out that Weeks had manhandled his daughter."

"Is that true, Miss Gordon?"

"Yes," Lisa said, snuffling. "Mr. Adams kept Weeks from striking me in the hotel lobby."

"The desk clerk can testify to that," Clint said.

"What else have you got to say?" Randle asked.

Clint studied Randle for a moment. With the

death of Gordon—one of the men Randle was afraid of—Randle seemed to be a bit steadier. Clint thought that when he left town Randle might become downright brave.

"Weeks sent those three men to kill me," Clint continued, "and he had Dundee killed because he could have proved that once he remembered where he'd seen the dead man before."

"That all sounds nice and neat, Mr. Adams," Randle said, "but can you prove it?"

"I don't have to, Sheriff," Clint said, standing up and helping Lisa to her feet. "You do."

"And how am I supposed to do that?" Randle asked, also standing.

"Find Jack Weeks."

As Clint walked to the door, Randle said, "You can't be leaving town, Adams."

Clint turned and looked at the sheriff, who said, "I mean, M-mister Adams. You, uh, I mean—"

"The Gypsies will be leaving tomorrow morning, Sheriff," Clint said. "I'll be staying to help Miss Gordon get her father buried."

"The Gypsies can't leave," Randle said. "I ain't found out who killed Dundee."

"I told you who killed him," Clint said, "or had him killed. Just find Jack Weeks."

"I can't take your word for that, Mr. Adams," Randle said. "The people in this town are gonna want an accounting for Mr. Gordon. He was a very important man."

"And I guess that makes Miss Gordon here a very important lady, doesn't it, Sheriff? She owns the ranch now."

Randle looked at Lisa Gordon and said, "Well, I

reckon that's right, but Weeks is the foreman."

"He was," Lisa said. "He's fired."

"You don't know that he killed anybody."

"I know he was planning something," she said, "and it had to do with Clint and the Gypsies, and I know he put his hands on me. That's all I need to know. He killed my father, Sheriff, and if you don't find him, I'll have your job."

"Miss Gordon—"

"Good day!"

She went out the door and Clint looked at Randle.

"Did you call for that marshal?"

"I—haven't had a chance—"

"Well, you better make time now," Clint said. "That will at least show the townspeople that you're doing something."

Outside, Lisa sagged against Clint.

"Oh, Clint, what am I going to do now?"

"Just what you did in there," he said. "Straighten your spine and take care of business."

"What business?"

"Getting your father buried proper is the first line of business," Clint said, "and then hiring yourself a foreman so the ranch runs smooth."

"Would you take that job?"

"I'm sure you have a man on the ranch who will qualify," Clint said. "Fact is, you've got some men in town here who are probably waiting on Weeks. You'd better let them know that Weeks doesn't work for you anymore."

"Where would they be now?"

"Most likely the saloon," Clint said. "You'll impress them if you go over there now, barely an hour after your father's . . . death . . . and take charge."

"I suppose so," she said. "Will you come with me?"

"I'll walk over there with you," he said, "sure."

Jack Weeks watched from a rooftop as Clint and Lisa Gordon walked across the street to the saloon. He knew that Nelson and Kyle and the others were there. By now Adams had convinced Lisa that he had killed her father, which wouldn't have happened if the old man hadn't grabbed for his gun. Stubborn old cuss wouldn't even listen to what he had to say.

Weeks knew he was in trouble, but only if Adams could convince the sheriff that he had killed Gordon, had Dundee killed, and tried to have Adams killed.

And Adams couldn't do any of that if *he* was dead.

"Come in with me?" Lisa asked.

"No," Clint said, "I'll wait outside and listen."

He nodded to her encouragingly, and she went through the bat-wing doors. It took a few minutes, but the place finally quieted down enough for her to start talking.

Clint listened and thought she did real well. Her voice was shaky at the beginning but gained strength as she went along.

"Jack Weeks," she continued, "is no longer connected with the S&G ranch. Any job he may have you doing now has nothing to do with my ranch. Any man who is still here an hour from now is fired. The only business you should have is back on the ranch."

"Are you saying that we got to go back to the ranch now or be fired?"

"That's what I'm saying."

"That ain't fair," someone else said.

"It isn't fair that my father is lying over at the undertaker's with a bullet in his belly, but he is," she said.

"That's true," another man's voice said. "I'm going back to the ranch, boys. Let's help Miss Lisa out in her time of need."

There were some murmurs of assent and a general scraping of chairs on the floor as the men stood up.

"Don't worry, Miss Lisa," the same man said to her as he passed. "We'll help you out."

"I appreciate that—uh, what is your name?"

"Lansing, ma'am, Bob Lansing."

"Thank you, Mr. Lansing."

Clint moved away from the door as the men filed out, and he counted eight of them. Too bad he didn't know how many had come into town.

Lisa came out of the saloon, wiping tears from her eyes.

"You did fine, Lisa," he said to her. "Just fine."

"What do I do now?"

"Well, if I were you," he said, "I'd talk to that fella Lansing about being your foreman—at least for the time being. Seems he helped you out in there quite a lot."

"Now?"

"Sure, before he rides off. He can go back to the ranch and tell the others what you said, and some of the others can attest to the fact that you named him foreman."

"A-all right," she said.

He watched as she stepped off the boardwalk and approached the men, who were mounting their horses. All he had to do was keep her busy for a while, until she realized that she was strong enough to handle the situation.

# THIRTY-FOUR

Clint left Lisa at the undertaker's and walked over to the livery, to talk to Delilah.

"What happened?" she asked. "We heard a shot."

"Mr. Gordon's been killed."

She waited a beat, then asked, "Will they blame that on us too?"

"No," Clint said, "I figure Gordon's foreman, Jack Weeks, is good for it. The sheriff will be looking for him. You and your people better pull out of here tomorrow, before the townspeople get any ideas."

"And what about you?"

"I'll be staying a bit longer," Clint said, "to try to clear things up."

"Do they think you did any of it?"

"There'll be a federal marshal through here soon enough, and I'll explain the whole thing to him."

169

"Maybe we should stay—"

"We will leave in the morning," Armando said. He'd been standing aside, listening to the conversation. "If you wish to stay behind, Delilah, that is your decision."

She turned on Armando angrily, but he turned his back on her and walked to King Ivan's wagon.

"Go with your people, Delilah," Clint said.

She looked at him hopefully, but when he said nothing else, her shoulders slumped.

"Yes," she said, "I suppose I had better."

"I'll talk to you later," he said.

"I understand Mr. Gordon had a daughter?" Delilah asked as he was walking away.

"He did."

"Will you be helping her?"

"Yes," he said. "She's Julia's age, and she took a chance coming to town to warn me about Jack Weeks. She needs help."

"Well," Delilah said, "you helped us, so now I guess it is time for you to help someone else."

"Seems to be what I do," Clint said, "stick my nose in other people's business. Well, I'd better get over to the undertaker's."

"Will I see you . . . before we leave?" she asked.

He smiled and said, "You'll see me."

When he got to the undertaker's, Lisa had finished her business with Paul Fixx.

"All done?" he asked.

"I'm finished," Lisa said. "I guess I'd better get back to the ranch before it gets dark."

"I'll ride back there with you, Lisa."

"Will you stay with me?"

"No, I'll be coming back to town."

"You'll have to ride in the dark."

"I'll find my way," he assured her. "Come on, we'd better get started."

Jack Weeks watched Clint and Lisa mount their horses and ride out of town, toward the ranch. He got down off the roof he'd been hiding on for hours, got on his horse, and went over to the saloon. When the S&G men had filed out, he hadn't seen Nelson or Kyle leave. Could be they didn't see themselves working for a woman. Weeks would hire Nelson and Kyle himself. Chances were that without Clint Adams around he might be able to get his—and their—jobs back.

When he had Nelson and Kyle, he'd head on out toward the ranch. He wasn't going to make any trouble on the way there, but when Clint Adams started riding back, he was going to find it a longer trip than he expected.

# THIRTY-FIVE

When Clint and Lisa rode up to the Gordon house, there was a man waiting there to take their horses.

"My name's Jenkins, Miss Gordon," he said. "Lansing told me you'd be along, wanted me to take care of your horse."

"Thank you, Jenkins," she said, dismounting. "It will just be my horse. Mr. Adams is returning to town."

"Yes, ma'am."

Jenkins took the horse and walked it to the barn.

"Looks like you're going to do all right, Lisa," Clint said.

"I'd be doing better if the sheriff would find Jack Weeks."

"He will," Clint said, "or the marshal will."

"Or you?"

"I might."

"I'd pay you well if you did, Clint," she said, "and if you killed him."

He hesitated a moment, then said, "My gun is not for sale, Lisa."

"I'm sorry," she said, and looked as if she were going to start crying. "I didn't mean to—"

"It's all right, Lisa," Clint said.

"Will you be back this way, Clint?"

"I'll make a point of passing by on my way out of town, Lisa."

"When will that be?"

"A couple of days, I guess."

"I'll be waiting."

"You'll be all right, Lisa. You'll be fine."

Clint turned Duke and started back to town.

"Are you sure killing Adams is gonna get you your job back, Jack?" Nelson asked.

"And when I get mine back, you get yours."

"Somebody's comin'," Kyle said.

"Get ready," Weeks said. "I'm moving to the other side of the road."

"We're ready," Nelson said.

Clint was thinking about Lisa when suddenly Duke stopped.

"What is it, big boy?" Clint asked, patting the gelding's huge neck. "What do you smell?"

Duke tossed his head and shook it from side to side.

"Whatever you smell," Clint said, "it spells trouble. Let's get off the road."

He took Duke off the road and started riding parallel to it. The moon was bright enough for him to see, and he saw two men on horseback waiting behind a stand of trees—the same ones he had waited behind for Lisa Gordon.

He halted Duke and dismounted, approaching the men on foot. He took out his gun and cocked the hammer.

"You boys waiting for someone?"

Both men stiffened.

"Dismount and toss your guns aside."

Neither man moved.

"Do it!"

Slowly they dismounted, but as they were about to discard their guns there was a shot, and something tugged at Clint's left sleeve.

The two men took advantage of the situation to draw their guns, and as Clint threw himself to one side he snapped off a shot. The bullet hit Kyle square in the chest and knocked him flat.

Clint landed hard on the ground and kept rolling, looking for cover. When he stopped, he looked around, but all he saw was the body of the man he'd shot.

"My guess is, that's you out there, Weeks," Clint said. He touched his arm and saw that he'd sustained a scratch that was bleeding worse than the wound was. "You hurried your shot, Weeks. Too bad. That's the only free one you get."

There was no reply.

Clint figured there were two men out there and they'd be positioning themselves to get him into a crossfire. If he stayed where he was, they'd have to do all the moving. It would be a lot of hours before daylight, and he didn't think they'd be that patient.

He rolled over onto his back, ejected the spent shells from his gun and reloaded, then settled down to wait.

Weeks wasn't sure what to do. He didn't think Clint Adams had gotten both Nelson *and* Kyle, but he was too good not to have gotten one of them. That meant that it was two against one, only he had no contact with the other man.

He hoped that whoever it was—Nelson or Kyle —the man didn't make any foolish moves.

Nelson couldn't wait any longer.

He hadn't heard Weeks or Clint Adams move in over an hour, and he couldn't wait any longer.

He got up in a crouch and started inching his way forward.

Clint heard someone moving around and got up on his knees to peer over the rock behind which he was hiding. He saw a man moving toward him in a crouch and trained his gun on him.

"Right there!" he shouted, but instead of moving, the man raised his gun and fired blindly. Clint fired once, striking the man in the torso. The man grunted and fell to the ground.

"Just you and me, Weeks!" Clint shouted. "It's just the two of us now. How you want to play this?"

Clint listened for a reply, and when it finally came, it wasn't the one he had anticipated. He heard the sound of a horse, moving toward town.

Weeks was running.

Clint stood up and checked the other two men. They were both dead. He went to where he'd left Duke, mounted up, and took off after Weeks.

He wondered if the man even knew the direction in which he was running.

# THIRTY-SIX

Jack Weeks rode into Virginia City on a dead run and continued that way until he reached the livery. He rode up to the Gypsy wagons, drew his guns, and started firing at the wagons. Only the fact that the wagons had wooden sides kept the people inside from being killed.

"Come on out, Gypsies," Jack Weeks called. "Come out . . ."

Clint rode into town wondering if Weeks had stopped there or just bypassed it. As he reached the sheriff's office he saw Sheriff Randle out front with Armando and Julia.

"What's the matter?" he asked. "What's wrong?"

"It's Weeks," Randle said.

"He took Delilah," Julia said.

"Where?"

"He's holed up in the livery with her," Randle said. "He's asking for you."

Clint looked up the street toward the livery, then dismounted.

"Sheriff, have you got an extra gun?"

"Sure, but—"

"Get it for me."

"What are you going to do?" Armando asked.

"If he's asking for me," Clint said, "he's going to get me."

Clint walked to the front of the livery and saw that the doors were closed.

"Weeks? Are you in there?"

"I'm in here, Adams," Weeks called back, "and I've got your Gypsy girlfriend."

"Let her go, Weeks," Clint said. "It's me you want, and I'm here."

"Come on in, Adams," Weeks said, "I'm waiting for you."

"Are you going to let him go alone?" Julia asked Sheriff Randle.

"It's his fight," Randle said.

"That man Weeks is a killer," Armando said. "That makes him your responsibility. If you let Adams die, I will tell everyone you were a coward."

Randle frowned, then started walking toward the livery.

"I don't need a couple of Gypsies to tell me my job," he muttered.

Clint went to the front doors and found them unlocked. He opened one enough to slip inside. The place was lit by a single storm lamp near the back.

"Walk into the light," Weeks called out.

Clint moved forward until he was inside the circle of light thrown by the lamp.

"Stop," Weeks said.

He stopped.

Weeks stepped out from a stall with Delilah held in front of him. He was pointing his gun at Clint.

"You've cost me everything I had," Weeks said.

"I did? I was the one who told you to kill people?"

"I didn't kill anyone."

"No, you just had people do it for you."

"I was doing what Sam Gordon wanted."

"But not the *way* he wanted it."

"He never told me how to do something, just to do it," Weeks said.

"Well, then maybe this is all his fault, but he's dead. You killed him."

"That was an accident. He grabbed for my gun and it went off."

"Look, Weeks, let her go—"

"Drop your gun, Adams."

"Weeks—"

"Drop it to the floor and kick it away, and I'll let her go."

"Clint, don't," Delilah said. "He'll kill you."

"Just stand easy, Delilah."

Clint eased his gun out of his holster, dropped it to the ground, and kicked it away.

"All right, Weeks," he said, spreading his hands, "now let her go."

"Sure," Weeks said. He'd had his arm across her chest, and now he moved it and pushed her away. "Now she can watch you die."

"Adams!" Sheriff Randle called out from the front door.

"Who's that?" Weeks demanded.

In that moment Delilah jumped him, banging into him with all her weight. He staggered and pushed her away from him.

Clint pulled the sheriff's extra gun from behind his back, where he'd had it stuck in his belt, and brought it to bear on Weeks.

"Weeks, don't—"

Weeks didn't listen. In a continuous move after pushing Delilah away from him a second time, he pointed his gun at Clint and pulled the trigger.

Clint pulled his trigger as he moved to one side. His bullet hit Weeks in the belly and the man staggered backward but did not drop his gun.

"Bastard!" he shouted, and tried to bring his gun up again.

Clint had no choice but to fire again, striking Weeks in the chest. This time the man dropped his gun and slumped to the floor.

Clint looked behind him to see where Weeks's shot had gone when it missed him and he saw Sheriff Randle on the floor of the stable.

"Randle! Where are you hit?"

He rushed to the sheriff's side and saw that the man was bleeding from the leg.

"You'll be all right."

"It hurts," Randle complained.

"Maybe it'll hurt less," Clint said, tying the sheriff's own bandanna around his leg, "if you think of it in terms of all the votes it will get you in the next election."

"Votes?"

"Sure," Clint said. "You took a bullet bringing in Sam Gordon's killer."

"Yeah, I did, didn't I?"

"You sure did."

Clint turned and stood up as Delilah came over to him.

"Are you all right?" he asked her.

"I'm fine. Is it finished now?"

"It's finished," Clint said, putting his arm around her. "You and your people can move on, Lisa Gordon can run her ranch, and I can go my way."

"And look for someone else to help?" she asked.

"I never look for people to help," he said, shaking his head helplessly. "They just seem to find me."

Watch for

**WAGON TRAIN TO HELL**

*ninety-ninth novel in the exciting*

*GUNSMITH series*

*coming in March!*

# J.R. ROBERTS
# THE
# GUNSMITH